PORTRAIT OF PARADISE

The lovely old manor house, Mallets, had been left to Katie's brother when their grandfather had died. Katie was thrilled when her brother asked her to go to Mallets to get things sorted out for his return to England. But it appeared that Ross Heseltine had already been put in charge of Mallets—and there Katie's problems began. It soon all seemed so hopeless to Katie, to find herself falling in love with the man who was quite obviously going to marry the very unpleasant Eve Clements...

PORTRAIT
OF PARADISE

Sue Peters

ATLANTIC LARGE PRINT
Chivers Press, Bath, England.
Curley Publishing, Inc.,
South Yarmouth, Mass., USA.

Library of Congress Cataloging-in-Publication Data

Peters, Sue.
    Portrait of paradise / Sue Peters.
        p.   cm.—(Atlantic large print)
    ISBN 0–7927–0353–7 (pbk.: lg. print)
    1. Large type books.   I. Title.   II. Series.
[PR6066.E747P6   1990]
823'.914—dc20   90–3446
                                                         CIP

British Library Cataloguing in Publication Data

Peters, Sue
    Portrait of paradise.
    I. Title
    823.914 [F]

    ISBN 0–7451–9891–0
    ISBN 0–7451–9903–8 pbk

This Large Print edition is published by Chivers Press, England, and
Curley Publishing, Inc, U.S.A. 1990

Published by arrangement with Harlequin Enterprises B.V.

U.K. Hardback ISBN 0 7451 9891 0
U.K. Softback ISBN 0 7451 9903 8
U.S.A. Softback ISBN 0 7927 0353 7

PORTRAIT OF PARADISE

CHAPTER ONE

'Mallets.'

It was an odd name for a house, reflected Katie. She smoothed out the solicitors' letter that had become crumpled from much reading, and looked again at the address.

'Mallets, Little Twickenham.'

She knew it off by heart, of course. There was no real need for her to read the cautiously worded note, phrased in the dry legal jargon that reduced her grandfather's death, and her brother's inheritance of his estate, to a routine matter or legal formality. The difficult bit lay in the last paragraph.

'It would greatly facilitate matters if you could see your way clear to return to England, and deal personally with ...' it finished pedantically. That meant her brother, of course, not herself. The letter had been addressed to Mark, she only carried it now as a sort of identity card, since the solicitor had no means of knowing who she was, except for the similar letter he had addressed to herself, informing her that under her grandfather's will she had been left the princely sum of fifteen hundred pounds, which she did not need, and, knowing her family background, she did not want to accept, either. But that was a minor hurdle, which she could jump later if necessary; the real difficulty was with Mark.

'I simply can't go,' he stated flatly. 'Jeremy Bailey, whoever he is,' the heading on the top of the solicitors' letter was Bailey, Bailey and Bailey, which sounded rather like three Army-type bridges, thought Katie irreverently, and the letter was signed by one Jeremy, senior partner. 'Jeremy Bailey will have to do the best he can, for a couple of months at any rate. Even when Wyn's had the baby,' he mentioned his prettily expectant wife, 'she won't be fit to travel for a few weeks,' he ran harassed hands through his hair, which was brown and wavy like Katie's own, but cut short, which robbed it of the gold tips that gave his sister's only slightly longer locks a shiny halo round her heart-shaped face, that was reflected in the light gold tips of her eyelashes, long enough to shade but not hide the pansy brown eyes underneath that were serious with concentration when she was engaged on her work, but could warm when she smiled in a way that lit the whole of her face.

'You go to England and I'll stay with Wyn,' suggested Katie. 'I haven't got anything planned at the moment, and I can keep myself free, it'll be a pleasant change to relax for a week or two.' She stretched lightly tanned arms above her head, and snuggled back contentedly in her chair.

'Leave Wyn—now?' Her brother turned shocked eyes in her direction. 'As if I could, while she's in this state!' he exclaimed, and his wife laughed.

'I haven't got the plague, darling.' She turned twinkling eyes at her sister-in-law. 'You can see it's our first baby,' she chuckled. 'I've never seen a husband in such a state!'

'It's all right for you, you're used to it,' her husband retorted, and the two women laughed outright.

'People could get the wrong impression, listening to you,' his wife scolded. 'It's a good job everyone knows I'm the local midwife,' she smiled.

'The local ex-midwife,' her spouse stated firmly, reaching out for the hand she held out to him. 'But if you're really free, Katie, why don't you go, and Wyn and I will join you later. And junior, of course,' he added carefully, trying the sound of his extended family and from the look on his face evidently liking it.

'Grandfather left the property to you, not to me,' began Katie doubtfully. 'I don't know if ...'

'It would be all right if you went with a letter of authority from me. I'd write to the solicitor and say you were coming,' he pressed his point, warming to the idea as he went along. 'It would solve Jeremy Bailey's problem, and mine, if you would act on my

3

behalf,' he urged her, 'and give you a holiday as well. I'd even pay your fare,' he grinned, knowing it to be unnecessary. Katie's skill as a portrait painter had made her much sought after by those wealthy enough to indulge their vanity in this direction, and financially independent for several years now, but Mark was as scrupulous about such matters as she, and Katie knew he would only accept her help on that condition. And he certainly looked as if he needed help now. Her normally self-assured relative had about him an air of strain that almost crackled, and which her sister-in-law assured her was normal with first fathers.

'Wait until we've had another four,' she said, unsympathetically, 'you'll be used to the routine by then.'

'Go and write that letter for me,' Katie cut across his groan, 'and I'll see what berths are available.' She turned to the telephone briskly, instantly glad of her decision as some of the cloud across her brother's face cleared. His letter was in her handbag now, ready to be presented as her credential to the unknown Jeremy Bailey, to whom her brother had also written separately, informing him that she was on her way. She did not know if Mark had received a reply from England, since the next morning a telephone call from the shipping office, offering her a last-minute cancellation on a boat due to sail on the evening tide, had sent her flying for the early train, minus most of the things she would probably want when she got to her destination, she thought philosophically, thankful for the first time for her own legacy since it would tide her over until she was able to sort herself out, and then, she told herself firmly, she would replace any of the money she spent and give the lot to some deserving charity.

Her nose wrinkled in distaste at the thought of touching any of her grandfather's money.

'It is hardly a sum to be trifled with, Miss Kimberley. Even in these days of inflation.' Jeremy Bailey regarded his visitor over the tops of his rimless glasses, which seemed to merge into his high, receding forehead and shiny bald cranium as if they grew there, thought Katie fascinated. His look was not disapproving, exactly. More—remote. She clutched at the word. So impersonal as to be almost not there. His thin, bony hands, covered by the parchment-like skin that looked as if it could be written on like one of his legal documents, fussed for a moment with her brother's letter. She knew it must be the one Mark had written to him, because she recognised his writing, and the date on the top coincided with the day before her hasty departure.

'I'd like to draw on it for necessary

expenses only, until I can get some of my own money transferred,' she told the solicitor forthrightly. 'As soon as I've done that, I'll make good what I've spent, and see you about disposing of the rest.' He would know of any deserving local charity, and so far as she was concerned he could handle the matter for her, she thought, but she did not say so at this juncture. Oddly enough, she felt herself liking this little, dried-up, mummy-like person, who had received her into his dusty, incredibly cluttered office and before he had spoken a word of business had shaken her hand with a firm grip and offered her a cup of tea. It had arrived accompanied by slender slices of sponge sandwich, and thin, sweet biscuits that made her forget how long it had been since she had her lunch. They were satisfying for all their thinness, and she munched happily, more at her ease when the elderly solicitor reached out with an unexpected twinkle, and confessed to a school-boy liking for what was evidently his afternoon treat.

He's human! Katie realised with relief, and settled back in her chair with a smile in his direction that had made friends for her in places all over the globe, and disposed of her need for an interpreter even when the language difficulties could not be overcome by her fluent French and rather more shaky German.

'You seem—er—reluctant to accept your legacy.' Jeremy Bailey spoke carefully, choosing his words, but obviously encouraged by his visitor's smile. 'Few people I know would refuse such a windfall ...' His voice lifted in a questioning note, leaving the sentence in mid-air for Katie to add to if she wished, or ignore as the spirit moved her.

'I'm one of the few.' She threw aside her scruples under the influence of the biscuits, and allowed her feelings to show, which they did perhaps more than she was aware of, the cloud across her mobile features betraying her thoughts to the eyes of the man opposite to her, that had surveyed much of the deviousness of human nature in a long lifetime of sorting out the tangles it left behind.

'You never met your grandfather.' As the family solicitor enjoying the close confidence of her deceased relative, he did not need to make it a question.

'No.' Katie's tone was short, and she checked herself hastily. It was not the fault of her companion that their family was divided. She leaned back in her chair again, making herself relax, deliberately unwinding the tight knot of anger that discussion on this subject always left inside her. 'Neither Mark nor I ever saw him,' she enlarged, 'but I think you know that.' Her smile was met by his nod, which made him rather like a Chinese

7

mandarin, she thought, except for his formal mode of dress, which despite being extremely old-fashioned, somehow suited him, she decided. 'Mother came back to England to see him once, some years ago now. I think you wrote telling her he was ill, or something.' She lifted questioning eyes to his.

'That is so. Your grandfather had a severe heart attack, and I thought it advisable to let your mother know, despite his instructions to the contrary.' So this little, formal man was quite capable of doing what he thought was right, even if it meant offending a wealthy client, thought Katie approvingly, liking him even more.

'Mother came, and Grandfather refused to receive her,' she said flatly, telling him nothing, she was sure, that he did not already know.

'It was—unfortunate,' Jeremy Bailey acknowledged with another mandarin-like nod.

'It was worse than that.' Anger vibrated through Katie's soft voice, making her face flush and her brown eyes spark. Making her prettier, if possible, than she already was, with a show of spirit that was not unlike her grandfather, a fact recognised by the elderly eyes opposite to her, that knew her background better even than Katie knew it herself. 'I heard her cry when she came back home.' Her voice was husky, memory making

8

her own eyes moist. Although it was a number of years now since they had lost their parents, she and Mark had never ceased to miss them.

'Your grandfather was a bitter man.' The quiet, pedantic voice held a note of compassion, but whether for the girl or his late client it was hard to tell. 'And a very unhappy one,' he added gently, holding Katie's startled look with his own serious one. 'During the last few years he mellowed a good deal,' he told her quietly. 'I think if your mother could have come to him then ... but of course, it was too late.'

''Flu epidemics don't wait for people to—mellow.' Katie's voice bit hardly.

'No,' the solicitor acknowledged, his expression regretting that bitterness should touch so young a voice. 'But remember he suffered too. He lost a great deal. By his own actions, I know,' he added hastily, hearing his visitor's sharp intake of breath. 'But he was very much against your mother and father marrying. He distrusted anyone who followed the arts for a living, and in his way a writer is as much of an artist as someone who paints,' he pointed out. 'Remember he was brought up to a rather more restricted choice of earning a living. He inherited the farm from his father, and he considered your father's means of livelihood to be feckless in the extreme.' His smile took the sting out of his

9

words. 'It was concern for your mother's well being that started the difficulty in the first place, and after that—well, your grandfather was a stubborn man,' he acknowledged. 'Even when it became plain that your father's work brought in a living far more comfortable than he himself could provide, he found it difficult—impossible—to retract.'

'In a way, he's done that now, I suppose,' Katie said thoughtfully. 'Mark's a writer. Did you know?' Another nod. 'And I'm a portrait painter,' she told him bluntly, 'so if there's a codicil or something in the will that debars people earning such a feckless living from being legatees, then all your trouble's been for nothing,' she finished, with a note in her voice that could have been hope. It was quickly squashed.

'There's nothing like that. In fact, your grandfather followed your brother's career with the utmost interest during the last few years of his life. After your parents died, that is.' He cleared his throat gruffly, with a tinge of anxiety in the look he threw in her direction, but she motioned him to go on, wondering what further surprises the dry, legal voice might give her. 'He read most of your brother's books. Even approved of them,' the parchment lips relaxed in a smile, 'and he knew, too, that your brother kept a small-holding as a hobby, to occupy his time when he wasn't writing.'

'Mark's got farming in his blood,' Katie said simply. 'We both have, I suppose, and it shows, though my efforts up to date have been confined to keeping chickens, and that didn't work out,' she admitted ruefully. 'When it came to killing them I found I couldn't eat them, so that ended that.'

'You travel a good deal?' The solicitor seemed to know a lot about her, as well, thought Katie shrewdly, reversing her description of him as a pinstripe-suited mandarin. He was more like a spider in the middle of a web, gathering information through the threads of this and that without those he gathered information about being aware even of his interest. A kindly spider, but...

'Yes, after the chicken incident I had a lot more commissions, so I took to living wherever my clients did. It seemed more convenient that way, and saved me the responsibility of having property to look after that was only used, perhaps, for a few weeks every year. In between times I stayed with Mark and his wife, and pottered about on their land. That way I could satisfy my liking for the life without having to know too much about it,' she smiled.

'Your brother's farm isn't extensive?'

'Heavens, no!' Katie laughed. 'It isn't a farm at all, really. He's only got a few fields round his house, he keeps a couple of goats to

11

supply them with milk, and a few fowl and things—that's about all he's got time for, although I know he'd like to extend his interests in that direction if he gets a chance.' Now that Mark was making a good income he could afford to indulge his hobby. 'If he did, though, he'd want his own land,' she went on. 'The holding he's got now is a rented one.'

'In that case, his legacy should be most acceptable.' The old voice was dry, and surprisingly the pale eyes twinkled behind the glasses. 'You didn't know Mallets was still a farm?' He viewed his visitor's surprise with raised eyebrows.

'No.' Katie looked puzzled. 'I thought Grandfather had sold off the land after Mother left home. They never talked about Mallets,' she said thoughtfully, 'it always upset Mother, so the subject was taboo at home. It had been an extensive place from the little I heard about it, but I thought there was just the house left, now?'

'The house and about fifty acres of land in all. Your grandfather kept some land, enough to occupy him without being too great a drain on his energy, and of course the land he sold provided more than enough capital to enable him to keep Mallets itself in excellent repair. Your brother has inherited a fine property,' he said appreciatively, 'it's in excellent running order, the only thing it lacks is a master.' Was there just the hint of reproach in his voice?'

'Well, I'm here to deputise for Mark until he can come himself.' Katie stirred and sat up. She had not taken the precaution of booking a hotel anywhere, assuming that this would be seen to by the solicitor, although she had hoped to be able to stay in her grandfather's house, as it would be so much more convenient than unpacking and having to pack again. She suddenly felt tired of moving around. It would be good to settle in one place for a couple of months. She would forget painting while she was at Mallets, she decided, and have a real holiday. Her last commission had been an exacting one, that of painting the portrait of a high-ranking government official in a country that was on the verge of a political takeover by a rival party. It had been a nerve-racking assignment, her own position an uneasy one, since she was a foreigner to whom civil strife might spell untold danger, and with this in the forefront of her mind she worked unceasingly to finish the portrait, and hoped when it was done that it might not be the last picture ever made of the ruler she had learned to like during his sittings, though the strain he was living under showed in the finished painting, however hard she tried not to let it.

'I don't know about deputise ...' The solicitor eyed her doubtfully.

'Oh, I don't mean cope with the farm,' Katie laughed outright. 'I shouldn't even know where to begin. There must be someone who does the work, though. You said Mallets was in excellent running order,' she reminded him.

'And so it is.' Another nod. 'So it is.'

Does he have to repeat everything he says? thought Katie with a flash of vexation that she knew was grossly unfair, but she felt travel-stained, and wanted a wash and brush up, and it would help to know where she was to dine and sleep that night.

'Then all that it needs until Mark can come and take over is someone to keep a general eye on things,' she said blithely. 'Someone to pay the bills and order whatever has to be ordered for sheep and cows and things.' She hadn't the vaguest idea what had to be ordered, but there must be something, and she had come all this way specially to do it. She smiled brightly at Jeremy Bailey and tried to look confident and knowledgeable, but her look could not have been very convincing because it failed to remove the doubtful frown from his forehead. 'Is anything the matter?' The hint of confusion—in anyone other than the senior partner of Bailey, Bailey & Bailey she might have said embarrassment—penetrated her consciousness and she stopped. 'If you're worried about a hotel room for me, I'm not fussy if it's only the village pub for a night or two,' she suggested the only problem that she could think might be worrying him.

'Hotel room? My dear Miss Kimberley,' he looked suitably scandalised, 'there's no question of booking you a room in an hotel, in the village or otherwise. You're expected at Mallets.' He made it sound as if she was expected at the Palace, she thought amusedly, but was careful not to interrupt him to say so. 'A room's been prepared for you, and I'll take you there myself,' he told her, with an old-fashioned assumption that an escort was necessary. Katie found his olde-worlde courtesy pleasant and rather refreshing. She had always frankly enjoyed being a girl.

'Then what . . . ?'

'Well—really—when Mr Kimberley wrote to say his sister would be coming in his stead—and knowing you were an artist . . .' To Katie's delight a dawning blush made Jeremy Bailey's parchment face quite rosy. 'I didn't expect such a capable young lady,' he confessed, and now embarrassment would be the correct description. Hearty embarrassment.

'You mean you thought all artists were vague creatures who fluttered about in pale draperies,' Katie accused him, with a chuckle which turned into a laugh at his patent look of relief at the way she had taken his halting explanation. 'I admit I'm a bit scatterbrained

15

at times,' her brother said most of the time, but brothers are nearly always unjust, 'but I'm normal enough, really,' she assured him.

'I can see you are,' he smiled, and relaxed. 'but you can imagine my predicament. A farm must have skilled hands to run it, and a master who is knowledgeable of its needs, and the way things should be done.'

'That's Mark,' his sister nodded.

'But Mark won't be coming for maybe two months,' the dry voice pointed out. 'So I accepted the offer of help from a local landowner who knew your grandfather well. He was in something of a predicament himself, and so we were able to temporarily solve one another's problems,' he said obliquely.

'You mean he feeds the hens and things.' Katie sounded as vague as his classic idea of an artist.

'Indeed I do not,' the solicitor protested. 'I mean he does the ordering—signs the cheques, and so on. There are farmhands to do the manual work,' he said rather stiffly.

'Sign the cheques?' Surely no one except Mark should do that, thought Katie, and as usual something of her feelings must have shown in her face.

'I have vested in Ross Heseltine the authority to manage Mallets until the formalities are completed, and your brother finally takes charge,' the solicitor replied.

'That entails committing the estate to any necessary expenditure to keep the place running. The amount of money he can use is restricted, of course,' he assured her hastily, his thin, bony fingers meeting in a steeple point above his blotting pad, once more the formal man of law. 'But I asked Mr Heseltine, as a favour to your late grandfather, to take charge of the farm, since I myself know little of the day to day running of such a holding.' The idea of Jeremy Bailey in anything so basic as gumboots and breeches brought a giggle to Katie's throat, which she hastily suppressed. 'I can hardly relieve him of his charge now ...' His voice trailed off, but left his meaning perfectly clear. That he had no intention of relieving the unknown Mr Heseltine of his charge, which nettled Katie somewhat, though her natural honesty made her admit—if only to herself—that he was probably justified in assuming she was not qualified to take charge, indeed she had openly admitted it herself, but just the same the nettled feeling remained.

'I see.' She did, too clearly. She was not only superfluous, she was an actual embarrassment, but now she was here she had no intention of going back until after Mark arrived.

'They'll make you very welcome at Mallets—as a guest, of course,' Jeremy Bailey hastened to make amends. 'Mr Heseltine is living there at the moment, since he was glad of temporary accommodation, so the arrangement suited us both. But I'm sure you'll get along famously.'

I wonder if we shall? thought Katie, taking refuge in formalities, and 'how d'you do-ing' the man whom the solicitor an hour later introduced as 'Mr Ross Heseltine, of the Lodge,' wherever the Lodge might be. At least he wasn't described as Ross Heseltine of Mallets, which was a relief after what Jeremy Bailey had told her, she thought tartly. His manner had implied that the man he had placed in charge of her grandfather's property might be an immovable fixture.

'How d'you do, Miss Kimberley?' he retaliated. He had the handsomest face she had ever seen, thought Katie. And the sternest. Perhaps stern wasn't the right word. Cruel? No, nor that either. Definitely not cruel. She searched for the right description, but it eluded her. His face was intriguing, to an artist, with the hint or arrogance in the high carriage of his head. His features were eminently paintable—as were Jeremy Bailey's, she told herself hastily. It was a good job she wasn't vulnerable to handsome faces, she thought; they were the norm rather than the exception in her work. This face wasn't merely handsome, though. It was—different. Dark, curling hair thickly crowned a high forehead, across which a freshly healed scar

18

that looked like a burn mark bit whitely into the deep tan of his skin. A pair of upward-curving lips took away the look that she had at first thought stern, and betrayed the smile that twinkled deep in the blue eyes that were studying her, she realised with a start, as closely as she was studying him.

'Perhaps you'd like to see your room?' he suggested after what seemed an endless minute, 'and then afterwards you can have a look round. We can talk after dinner,' he offered rather as if she had come for an interview, she thought sharply, but bit back her retort as he turned to the solicitor. 'What about you, Jeremy?' he turned courteously to the older man. 'Will you stay with us?'

'I'm afraid not tonight, I have an appointment,' the solicitor refused. 'I'll be in touch of course, Miss Kimberley, but if there's anything you want me for...'

'I'll give you a ring,' Katie assured him, with a confidence she was far from feeling. She wished suddenly that he had accepted the invitation to dinner. That she did not have to enter her grandfather's house alone. For she felt alone, since this dark-haired man of tall, strong build was a stranger, and one, moreover, with whom she did not feel the same rapport she had felt with the elderly solicitor, probably due to the faint, prickly feeling that this man, however unwittingly, had usurped her place at Mallets, and would remain there whether she liked it or not until Mark arrived and made Ross Heseltine's presence there as unnecessary as her own was now.

'This way.' He bent and picked up her suitcases from where the taxi driver had deposited them on the drive, at her own request since Ross Heseltine 'had strode to meet them across the lawn, coming from somewhere round the corner of the house at the sound of the taxi, which now bore the solicitor back to wherever his appointment happened to be. She watched it disappear round a corner of the long drive, and turned with a small sigh to follow her companion, who was watching her with narrowed eyes.

'It's your first time here, isn't it?' His deep voice was quiet, and she nodded, not resenting the question, which was kindly enough, with no hint of curiosity in it.

'Yes,' she nodded. She would have to stop that, she did not want it to become the mandarin-like habit that her recent companion had adopted. A kimono wouldn't suit her, she thought irrelevantly, trying with flippancy to quiet the tension that gripped her as she regarded her mother's old home. It was not a place anyone would want to leave, except for an all-important reason, she thought, understanding more fully her mother's distress at the separation, and her father's strict injunction to herself and Mark that they must never mention Mallets, or ask questions about it. They would learn all that was necessary when they were old enough to understand. It was the only real restraint that he had ever insisted on, and probably for that reason they were careful to obey him to the letter, so that Mallets, to them, had become a thing of fantasy, a fairytale castle inhabited by an ogre, and rarely thought of as they grew up, and the interest of their own lives claimed their sole attention.

Jeremy Bailey had been correct when he had said it was in excellent running order. White-painted fences served as boundaries to closely cropped green lawns, in which deep borders had been cut to accommodate the wallflowers that wafted heavenly perfume towards them on the late April breeze. The house itself was built of blocks of warm, cream-coloured stone that softened the rather uncompromising square shape of it, that she realised had distinct advantages when she walked through the panelled hall and into the light, airy drawing room that made spacious use of its shape, to the advantage of the solid, old-fashioned furniture that looked comfortably content to remain in its appointed place, where it had been for several generations, and saw no reason why it should not remain for several generations yet to come.

Everything seemed to belong, except

Katie.

'I'll go and find Amy, she'll show you to your room,' Ross Heseltine stuck his head through the door and called.

'Will I do? Amy's coping with a crisis in the kitchen.' A light, cool voice came from just outside the open french windows, its sound almost immediately followed by its owner, who appeared to rise from what must be a seat out of sight on the crazy paving area from which, here and there, bright clumps of spring flowering rockery plants made patches of colour to wander among. 'She set the gravy on fire. Oh, don't worry,' as the man made a concerned noise, 'the flames are out now, and no one's been scorched.' The amusement in her voice did not seem to reach the green eyes that looked Katie up and down with a calculating stare, which she did not bother to remove until a lock of her dark auburn hair, piled high on top of her head, fell loosely across her fragile cheekbones, which showed through skin of the transparent delicacy that so often goes with hair of that particular shade. 'I was on my way home,' she broke a rather uncomfortable silence, 'but I thought I'd look in to see if your—visitor—had come.' Was it Katie's imagination, or did she lay faint stress on the word 'visitor'? And if she was on her way home; as she said, what had brought her sitting outside the window, she must have heard the man talking, but it had

22

been several minutes before she made her presence known to the occupants of the room.

'Perhaps you'll show Miss Kimberley to her room, Eve.' Ross sounded relieved. 'You know which one it is...'

'Call me Katie,' Katie begged, suddenly sick of the formalities. 'It's quicker,' she said flatly. And Miss Kimberley makes me feel about ninety, she thought, but she did not say so, reluctant to give the owner of the green eyes a weapon that she was sure she would use if she knew it annoyed.

'In that case, my name's Ross, and this is Eve—Eve Clements,' Ross introduced the auburn-haired newcomer. 'Eve runs a riding school, she rents one of the fields on Mallets.'

'I'm part of the establishment, so to speak,' the other girl murmured, in what to the man's ears probably sounded a friendly voice, but to Katie's sensitive lobes sounded the reverse of welcoming. 'Here's your room. It's the guest bedroom.' This time there was no mistaking the emphasis, any more than Katie realised she could refute her claim. The girl seemed to know the run of the house off by heart, as if she was indeed part of the establishment. She wondered if it had been so when her grandfather was alive, or only since Ross took over the management of the farm. If the man was a friend of her late relative's, it was quite possible the girl was too. He must have had some friends, thought Katie grudgingly; the opinion she and Mark had of him need not necessarily be shared by the rest of the universe. 'That sounds as if someone's brought up your cases—oh, it's you, Ross,' she opened the door and beckoned him inside as he hesitated. 'Now you've brought the cases up I'll leave—er—Katie—to unpack.' Surely she hadn't forgotten her name already, Katie thought, picking up the deliberate hesitation. Eve Clements did not look the sort of person who would forget anything easily, there was sharp intelligence behind the green stare. She was a beautiful woman, thought Katie critically, but there was a lack of something—a shallowness, perhaps—that made her face uninteresting to Katie the artist, as her manner made her repelling to Katie the person, she admitted ruefully.

'Thank you for these,' she smiled at Ross, indicating the two heavy cases that he had swung on to the flat top of a huge blanket chest at the foot of her bed as if they were no heavier than a child's satchel.

'Now I've done the honours,' Eve put a slender hand on the door handle, preparatory to making her departure. She did it with calculating effect, turning back to face the other two, so that the dark wood of the door outlined her slender figure, already shown to advantage by the perfectly cut jodhpurs and the rather too well fitting, open-necked cream shirt. 'Now I've done the honours, I'll make my way to my own lonely dinner. I'll leave you to cope—darling,' she smiled at Ross, and tripped lightly away. Katie could hear her feet tap on the polished wood block floor of the hall, and her light voice calling goodnight to someone—a man, from the sound of the reply—outside the front door. Ross spoke to the same person, Katie could hear them in conversation as she turned to her suitcases, shutting the door with a determined self-restraint that would not let her slam it behind them as she felt inclined. Ross hadn't invited Eve to dinner. She wondered if he would have joined her at her own home if he hadn't had to entertain a visitor to Mallets. Eve had said she would leave him to cope, as if she was some sort of problem instead of a person, thought Katie furiously—and admitted with ruthless honesty that to them she probably was. A problem that had to be coped with, and one that in all probability Ross, as well as Eve, did not particularly like.

CHAPTER TWO

She met Amy as she came downstairs.

The clatter of saucepans, a loud crash that sounded as if something had ended its useful life on the stone flags of a kitchen floor, and a

25

strong smell of dinner cooking brought Katie out of her room, fearful lest she be late for the evening meal on her first night in her grandfather's home. She would not admit to being a guest there, particularly Ross's guest.

'It's late, I'm afraid, miss.' A stout, fair-haired figure, with jumper sleeves rolled up over muscles that would not disgrace a man, and a round face that Kate judged in other circumstances might be cheerful, regarded her with a harassed expression. 'The gravy set on fire, so I had to start again.' Her cheeks were scarlet with the effort of starting again, and Katie smiled encouragingly.

'I'm sure we shall enjoy it all the more,' she said kindly, glad to find that there was someone else in the house besides herself at a disadvantage. 'You go ahead,' she waved the woman on, fearful for the tray load of vegetable dishes that slid on its shiny surface disconcertingly near the edge. 'You know the way to the dining room, I don't.'

'It's the door on the right, opposite the drawing room, miss.' The fair head nodded vigorously, and Katie thrust down a sudden desire to giggle. They were all at it, she thought hystericaly, and dived forward just in time as a large sandalled foot kicked at the indicated door and found it unexpectedly shut.

'You go first.' Katie's voice was firm; she would be glad to see the vegetable dishes

26

safely on the table. She followed the woman in, and turned as Ross spoke from the window.

'I see you've met Amy.' He strolled towards them. 'I'd better introduce you properly,' he smiled. 'Amy, this is Miss Kimberley. Katie, meet Mrs Dawson—Amy to the family.'

It was an unfortunate choice of words from Katie's point of view, and she felt herself bristle.

What on earth's the matter with me? she thought wonderingly. She did not usually react in this manner with other people, but it galled her to hear this man refer to himself as family. He was nothing of the sort. Not that she really wanted to be, herself. Neither she nor Mark had ever felt particularly proud of their link with Garfield Spurr, it was a relationship they themselves would rather have been without. She was like a dog in the manger, she thought guiltily; she didn't want it herself and resented other people laying claim to it.

'I'm right glad you've come, miss.' A pudgy hand, damp from much effort among the pots and pans, wrung her own with obvious sincerity, and Katie warmed to its owner. 'This place can do with a woman's hand, now that Mrs Morris has gone,' she explained seriously. 'I can cope with the plain stuff,' she told Katie confidently, 'but I'm not

27

much of a hand with anything fancy. My Ben, he only liked plain stuff. Good plain cooking, he calls it,' she said proudly.

'Who was Mrs Morris?' Katie surveyed the good plain cooking on her plate, and wondered how she was going to get through the overdone meat, underdone potatoes and soggy cabbage that lined her plate, surrounded with dubious gravy that at first taste told her it had been burned almost as badly as the original attempt.

'She was your grandfather's housekeeper.' Ross's eyes twinkled as he watched her pick at her food. 'He left her a small annuity, and when he died she went to live with her sister in Surrey. She was elderly herself, and glad to retire,' he told her.

'And Amy?'

'She and Ben Dawson live in, Ben copes with the outside work and Amy copes inside. Since Mrs Morris left she's done the cooking, though it's not very successful, I'm afraid,' he said gravely. 'She was originally engaged just for the housework, and she managed that extremely well.' Katie could see that; the whole place shone with elbow grease, which probably explained Amy's robust muscles. 'Don't worry, the cheese and biscuits are excellent,' he smiled.

'That's a relief.' Katie forked another mouthful, hesitated, and laid her utensils back on her plate.

'I swallow it rather than offend Amy,' Ross hinted. 'She's been an invaluable help, and her husband knows the running of the farm work inside out. Your brother will be glad to keep them, I expect,' he pressed his point, and Katie took up her fork again and plodded steadily through what suddenly seemed a mountain of vegetables. 'Amy's good with children, too,' Ross encouraged her. 'She's got none of her own, but the youngsters from the riding school find her a soft touch for glasses of lemonade and things,' he smiled, 'and she does nothing to discourage them.' He had a nice smile, thought Katie. Cheerful, as if it took a lot to upset him. It curved his lips and made tiny wrinkles round his eyes, touching the edge of the scar across his forehead that reached down to his temple. She wondered about the scar. It made him look slightly piratical, but she did not like to ask him how it had come about, as he might think it prying.

'Wyn might be glad of help with the baby when she arrives here,' she admitted, and found the thought helped her to finish the remainder of her dinner, even to accepting a helping of the dried-up rice pudding that appeared next. The cheese and biscuits made up in quality what the earlier courses had lacked, and the coffee, surprisingly, was quite good.

'Shall we drink it here,' suggested Ross,

29

'and then perhaps you'd like to look round outside before it gets dark. That is, if you're not too tired from your journey?' he said considerately.

'I'd like that,' she admitted. It would be good to get out of the house for a while; she did not feel at ease there. The shadow of the man she had never even met, but to whom she was tied irretrievably by blood relationship, loomed over it with a brooding unhappiness that disturbed her, sensitive as she was to the atmosphere of houses. Even if she had come to Mallets as a stranger, knowing nothing of their family history, she would have sensed the bitterness that seemed to emanate from the very walls. Some houses were happy houses, reflecting the contentment of their inhabitants, but Mallets was definitely not. It had about it a feeling of waiting, thought Katie. Perhaps waiting for the child who was not yet born, but whose tiny feet would trot along its corridors, and whose laughter would one day chase away the shadows that loomed as much in her own mind as in the house itself.

'I should slip on a coat, it goes chilly here at night,' Ross warned her, and she ran upstairs to her bedroom, shrugging herself into a fine wool camel travelling coat, but leaving the front open. She could close it later if she found herself getting cold. The pockets were slanted, and easy to thrust her hands into, and she followed Ross outside the front door, breathing deeply with the relief of being outside as much as with pleasure at the perfume of the wallflowers that rose like incense all round them.

'They're lovely, aren't they?' Her companion looked down at her consideringly, and spoke with deliberation. 'Your grandfather loved the old-fashioned flowers, you'll find bags of lavender in all the cupboards from that hedge over there,' he pointed to a deep hedge of the bushes lining a wall that marked the perimeter of the garden on the one side, and effectively separated it from the farmyard, and kept the working area well away from the extensive garden that surrounded the house. Katie paused and looked back at the house. It was just a building really, but ... Suddenly, she felt sorry for the house. Walls as warmly coloured as these should hold happy people, she thought; their very colour looked welcoming.

'It'll be better when Mark and his family come to live here.' She spoke half to herself, forgetting her companion, temporarily, so that she started when he spoke.

'The house will feel—' he hesitated, 'be a happier one,' he amended, and Katie looked up at him, surprised.

'You feel that, too?' They had been on the same wavelength, evidently, and she warmed towards him suddenly. It wasn't everyone who understood about houses having feelings ... The prickles that had made her regard the man beside her with suspicion before subsided a little. Not altogether, but enough to make her smile up at him. 'Having a child here—children,' she knew Mark and Wyn wanted more than one, 'will put things right—' She left her sentence in mid-air, oddly certain that Ross would understand.

'It's had children here. Your grandfather was fond of them, that was why he encouraged the formation of the riding school,' he said quietly, 'but of course none of them belonged.' He too left her to pick up his meaning, and for a brief second their eyes met in complete understanding, though she wished he had not mentioned her grandfather. After years of regarding him as an ogre, she was not sure that she wanted to get to know him—even posthumously—as a human being. 'It's better to leave the past behind,' he trespassed warily, patently uncertain of her reaction. 'Mallets has got a future, now,' he reminded her gently, sliding his hand under her elbow to guide her through a small wicket gate in the wall that led on to the farmyard. 'I expect you'd like to see the stock.' He tactfully turned the subject. 'They're interesting, just now,' he smiled, pausing with her as she stopped beside a hencoop with a gasp of delight at the fluffy yellow mites that ran under their mothers' wings for protection as they approached. 'We've had to coop them pretty firmly,' he explained the row of pens that held a miscellany of fowl, ending in one or two big ones that enclosed geese. 'We're troubled by foxes, the wolds are an ideal breeding place for them.' He waved his hand at the green, rolling slopes that were of a uniform, gentle roundness except for where a rugged outcrop of rock stood up starkly to the one side, as if resisting the growth of soft grass that greened the other slopes, remaining harshly aloof—almost like her grandfather, thought Katie, with un expected pang of pity for a fellow creature misguided enough to reject that which he loved most, thereby rejecting happiness as well, until it was too late to make amends.

'I'm not sorry you've penned that one!' She backed hastily as a large white gander hissed threateningly with extended neck, from the other side of the pen wire.

'He's an excellent watchdog when he's loose,' Ross laughed, catching her arm again in a friendly fashion, so that they walked closely together, Katie following his lead, content for the moment to be shown around. She could find her own way about later, she decided. 'That old gander is as good at keeping strangers at bay as any dog, even Glen.' He snapped his fingers as a tall, chocolate-coloured dog appeared from one of the sheds and looked towards them. 'Come on with us,' he invited, setting the plume of a tail waving happily.

'He's big, for a spaniel.' Katie fondled the soft droopy ears curiously.

'He's a spaniel-retriever cross, a good mixture for a gundog,' Ross explained. 'He can swim like a fish, and he's got a soft mouth for retrieving. He's mine,' he added, rather unnecessarily, since the dog's behaviour made it obvious whom it regarded as its master.

'Had Grandfather got a dog?' She had not seen one about the house, which seemed strange on a farm.

'Yes, he'd had a labrador, but it died a couple of months before he did,' Ross said evenly, respecting her desire to know without going into too much detail. 'It was very old, and as your grandfather was more or less confined to bed he didn't bother to get another.'

That disposed of one problem, at least, she thought, glad that the big brown dog did not belong to the farm. It was obviously devoted to Ross, and disputed ownership was a complication she felt she and Mark could do without. Mallets had been trouble enough in their lives without adding more, she thought, pausing as something stirred in the dusk of a nearby shed.

'Did he keep horses?' She peeped over the half door, and withdrew her head hurriedly as the occupant lifted a friendly muzzle almost in her face. 'Oh, it's . . .'

'It's a shorthorn bull,' Ross laughed at her hasty skip, and grasped her quickly round the waist as she lost her balance on the uneven cobbles. 'He won't hurt you, he's as gentle as a lamb,' he assured her. 'He's called Cup—short for Buttercup,' he added gravely.

'I can't think of anything less like a buttercup,' Katie declared, firmly keeping her distance as Ross reached out a hand and scratched the creature's nose.

'The colour's appropriate,' he said practically. 'He earns his weight in gold in stud fees. He's a pedigree,' he explained.

'Maybe that's why he gave me such a haughty look.' She was not convinced by the bull's mild manner. 'I'd rather admire him from a distance. I prefer Glen.' She reached down to touch the friendly nose raised up at the sound of the dog's name.

'Do you have a dog of your own?'

'No, I'd like one, but I travel about too much.' Katie leaned her arms reflectively across the top of the garden wall as they made their slow way back to the house, and crushed a stem of lavender between her fingers to breathe in the sharp, sweet scent of it, tucking the bruised leaves in her pocket to add their perfume to the handkerchief that lay folded there. 'Mark had one, but it got killed a few weeks ago by a car.'

'There would have been problems bringing a dog into England. Quarantine, and so on,' Ross pointed out.

'I know. In a way it's probably for the best,' she acknowledged. 'They wouldn't have wanted to let him go to a new owner, and six months in kennels wouldn't be much fun for a family pet, used to being fussed.'

'Why not get a dog while you're here, and house-train it for them before they come over?' Ross suggested idly, leaning beside her and surveying the slope of land rolling gently away from them.

'I could do that.' Dawning interest livened Katie's voice. 'It would be a nice idea, a sort of welcome home.'

'And company for you in the meantime,' Ross agreed. 'There's plenty of land where you can exercise a puppy.' He pointed downwards to where a narrow ribbon of water wandered in undecided loops and spirals at the lowest level of the fields. 'That's the Burley Brook,' he told her. 'It forms the boundary of the Mallets land that's left. When your grandfather sold the major part of his acreage he decided to keep the fields that lay on the house side of the brook, the watercourse made an easy boundary, and he used to say he could look over all his property from his own garden,' he added with a reminiscent smile.

That wouldn't be difficult, realised Katie.

Mallets stood on the crown of a small hill, and from the garden her grandfather would be literally owner of all he surveyed—if not quite king, she added to herself drily. But of course the autocratic old man had discovered that, to his cost, when he found he could not rule his own daughter, so in royal fashion he had banished her.

'I'll see what I can do.' Ross's voice recalled her to what he was saying. 'About a dog for you,' he reminded her, meeting her blank look.

'Oh—yes, thank you.' She shivered, and drew her coat more closely about her.

'Would you like to go in?' Instantly he straightened up from the wall.

'Not just yet.' She felt childishly reluctant to return to the house, and the isolation of her bedroom when the lights were put out. 'What about the land on the other side of the brook?' She wasn't really interested, but it put off going indoors, and she pointed to the rich green meadows that invited a walker with their lush softness.

'That used to belong to Mallets.' Ross resumed his former stance, and gazed in the direction she pointed at. 'It's part of the land belonging to the Lodge, now,' he told her. 'But you can walk there, too, if you want to,' he went on quietly. 'The—owner—wouldn't mind.'

It was only afterwards, in the solitude of

her room, with the light out, and the moonlight softening the heavy outlines of the old-fashioned funiture, that she realised he had said the land on the other side of the brook belonged to the Lodge. Jeremy Bailey had introduced him as Ross Heseltine of the Lodge, she remembered, and Ross had said the owner wouldn't mind her walking there as if he was certain of that owner's permission. Perhaps he had only bought a field or two, and the rest had been split up among other landowners on the boundaries of Mallets, but even a field or two would be costly, she realised. The solicitor had described Ross as a local landowner, and a friend of her grandfather's. But if he was local, why did he not go home at night instead of staying at Mallets? Jeremy Bailey had said he was glad of temporary accommodation. It all seemed very confusing, but no doubt there was quite a simple explanation, she thought, turning restlessly between sheets that, as Ross predicted, smelled faintly of lavender.

She thought of her dog instead. What sort would he be? she wondered. She would have to find him a suitable name. She smiled into the dusky room, letting her mind dwell on the pleasant problem, glad of its distraction to release her from the pent-up feelings that had lain heavily across her from the time she had first offered to come to Mallets. Perhaps it would be a spaniel-retriever, like Glen. The big chocolate brown dog had a gentle way with him that was instantly attractive, but he was tall for a house pet. No, a smaller dog would be better, she decided dreamily. Perhaps she wouldn't have a choice. Ross said he would see what he could do. It was spring, so he might know of a litter of pups somewhere. She would enjoy walking in the fields if she had a dog for company, she thought, and remembered Ross's comment on that subject, too. He had said the dog would be company for her. Which looked as if her feeling of being an unwelcome guest in her late grandfather's house might have some foundation in fact, she thought ruefully. As if Ross might prefer her to have some kind of company, any kind, that would relieve him of the responsibility of being a companion to her himself.

The thought of Eve Clements came to her, and she shook her head. Eve and she would be no company for one another, she decided, remembering the girl's calculating stare, and her insistence on being part of the household, a deliberate ploy to make Katie herself feel an outsider, although she was the only one of them who was 'family', she thought, a flick of anger making her sit up in bed and unnecessarily pummel the pillows into a more comfortable shape behind her. To be fair, her arrival could have upset the others' plans, although she had not come upon them

39

unexpectedly; they had had warning of her coming, and if she had not arrived then her brother would have done if circumstances had been more favourable, so what was the difference? she wondered. Except that, if she had not been in to dinner, Ross would probably have had his meal with Eve, and spent a more enjoyable evening than he had escorting herself round her brother's inheritance. Certainly he would have had better food, she grinned to herself, remembering his heroic attempts to look as if he enjoyed the ill cooked repast in order to encourage her to eat her own.

That's something I can alter, though I'll have to do it tactfully, she told herself. Years of living out of a suitcase had made her adept at quick, tasty meals, and she had no intention of suffering Amy's 'good plain stuff' for a moment longer than she could help—it was gastronomic suicide. She let her mind roam lazily over the possibilities for the first meal she would cook here. It would be a pleasant surprise for Ross. The thought that her cooking might please him gave her spirits an unexpected uplift. She would look round the house tomorrow, and investigate the kitchen quarters in the process. It would not look so obvious, then. She prepared her plan of campaign. She could see what sort of cooker they had. Electric, or gas or—her spirits yo-yoed back again to their former level as she realised with a feeling of foreboding that they might—just might—cook by means of an old-fashioned solid fuel range, in which case her best efforts would probably be no better than those of the unfortunate Amy.

By breakfast time she felt more cheerful. Amy brought her up a cup of tea just as she woke about seven o'clock, which she didn't expect, and she smiled at the woman in honest gratitude for her kindly thought.

'Me and Ben 'as one first thing, and so does Mr Ross, so I thought I'd bring you one up.' Amy seemed inclined to be friendly, thought Katie with relief, and voiced her appreciation with such sincerity that it brought a beam to the chubby face, and visibly relaxed the slight wariness that Katie had sensed in her before. Amy had regarded her in much the same manner as she herself had regarded the shorthorn bull, testing the temperature before committing herself.

Well, she knows I won't bite, thought Katie, shaking cornflakes on to the blue and white dish she found in her place at the table. There was nothing Amy could do to cornflakes, she thought thankfully, and at least she managed drinkable coffee.

'Don't wait for Mr Ross, miss,' Amy advised her when she first got down. 'He an' Ben will come in when they've done in the yard,' and she left her to finish her meal in peace. It was another twenty minutes before Ross appeared, by which time Katie had walked her cup of coffee right round the room while investigating its contents, and the view from the window, which looked out on to the lavender hedge she had robbed the night before. The perfume from the lavender would later in the year blow into the dining room just as the perfume from the wallflowers made the air of the drawing room sweet now, she thought appreciatively, pausing in front of a rather nice print hung on the wall. She peered closer, and discovered it to be signed. Her grandfather might not have approved of people who followed the arts for a living, she thought, but he had a discriminating eye for their output. Or maybe the picture had been purchased before his time. Garfield Spurr had followed a long line of those who carried his name and farmed this land, just as Mark would follow him now, though his name was Kimberley, not Spurr. She felt suddenly relieved that there would be a new name at the head of this house. It would be like a new start, she thought, wiping away any shadows from the past, and giving their son—Wyn had been sure the new arrival would be a boy—a new, bright sheet to map his future on, unfettered by ties from the past.

'Sorry I'm late. I see Amy told you not to wait.' Ross slid into his chair, and Katie returned to the table and poured him out a cup of coffee. 'Thanks.' He looked surprised, and then his blue eyes twinkled in a pleased fashion. 'One of the hands is off sick, so I'm giving Ben a hand first thing with the stock,' he explained. 'That reminds me,' he spoke abstractedly, 'I must remember to tell Ben about those sacks of feed, they've sent the wrong mixture ...' He began on his breakfast purposefully, with the air of a man who has no time to waste, and Katie lapsed into silence until they were disturbed by Amy bringing in two boiled eggs. 'Amy boils eggs beautifully,' he looked across the table at Katie as the door shut behind the reluctant cook. 'They're done to a turn,' he said gravely, and she twinkled back at him.

'She doesn't seem too happy with her new responsibilities.'

'She isn't,' he confirmed. 'Amy likes "doing out" the house. She cleans and polishes, and everything shines. Including you if you get in the way of her duster,' he said ruefully, and Katie chuckled, enjoying the picture of the all-powerful Ross Heseltine flying before the onslaught of the domestic machinery.

'I thought I might be able to help out, there ...' She didn't quite know how to put it, for Mark's sake she did not want to upset Ross any more than she wanted to upset Amy. She would eventually leave and take up the threads of her life after Mark took over, but her brother and his family would have this man as a neighbour, and it was obviously better if they were on friendly terms from the start, and she herself would have to live in close proximity to him until her brother arrived and released her from her charge. The fact that neither the solicitor nor Ross seemed to regard it as her charge, but his, still galled her, but it was something she must learn to live with, so she might as well live in peace, since it was only for a short time anyhow, she thought sensibly.

'Can you cook?' He regarded her in frank surprise, his spoon half way to his mouth, and threatening to drip on to his sweater if he did not attend to its contents.

'You're losing the yolk!' Katie could stand the suspense no longer, and watched the spoonful of egg disappear intact into his mouth with a feeling of relief. 'Of course I can cook,' she retorted indignantly. 'Everyone can. Perhaps not everyone,' she amended, as his eyes glinted. 'I shall have to be careful, though, I don't want to offend Amy.' She looked her doubt, her eyes seeking his. For permission? She didn't want his permission, she told herself firmly, but just the same she was glad when he nodded, his mouth too full for the moment to make speaking practical.

'You won't offend Amy,' he smiled after a minute, 'she's only doing it to oblige. Yes, oblige,' he repeated with emphasis as Katie's eyebrows rose in a questioning arc. 'So far as she's concerned, cooking's a waste of time. She says she's no sooner made something than it disappears, so why bother in the first place?'

'In that case I'll go and search her out and have a look at the facilities. I suppose you don't . . .'

'No, I don't,' he retorted. 'I rarely enter the kitchen quarters, so she might be using a log fire on the doorstep for all I know. Now and then I've suspected she might have done just that,' he said ruefully, and Katie laughed. 'She and Ben will have finished their meal by now, why don't you go and see her right away?' he said encouragingly. 'And if Ben's there, ask him to pop in and see me before he does anything else, will you?' he asked her. 'I want to have a word with him about those bags of feed.'

He didn't suggest she remain to discuss the bags of feed, and Katie hesitated for a moment, then with a shrug she decided not to press the point, for the moment anyhow, and turned instead towards the door, aware of Ross's questioning look as he saw her pause, but ignoring it, and closing the door behind her before he could speak.

'Has Mr Ross finished his breakfast, miss?' Amy's head appeared through the kitchen door at the end of the passage, and Katie

45

turned towards her, glad of the opening for her own intended inspection of the domestic quarters.

'Not quite, he's just finishing his coffee,' she answered, 'but he's asked if your husband could go and see him—oh, Mr Dawson,' as a burly, balding figure in rolled-up shirt sleeves and faded blue overalls appeared, 'would you pop in and see Mr Heseltine, please, before you start anything else? He wants to see you about some bags of feed.' She smiled at him in a friendly fashion as he nodded an inarticulate 'Marnin'' and stood aside for her to go through the kitchen door.

'It's a bit untidy, miss,' Amy looked doubtfully around her domain. 'I was just waiting to start on the washing up when Mr Ross had finished with his crocks.'

'It looks all right to me.' Katie looked round at the well scrubbed apartment. If their food was ill cooked, she thought, she would have no doubts about its cleanliness. The whole place shone, as did Amy herself, and for that matter Ben too—she smiled as she recalled his well polished look. The deep porcelain sink was neatly stacked ready for the washing up, and the grate shone.

The grate ... Katie regarded it with dismay. A red fire was already burning there, and from the number of trivets and hooks festooning the front bars there was no longer any doubt in her mind that it was put to

46

regular use by Amy.

'Do you cook on—that?' She pointed at the grate, and Amy nodded brightly.

'Oh yes, miss, it's just like the one me mum had. She lives in one of them cottages along the High Street,' she smiled. 'Saved my bacon, this did, when Mrs Morris left, and I had to do the cooking. I was used to a grate like it, see? And I couldn't seem to get along with that thing nohow.' She moved a laden clothes-horse from in front of something that stood nearby, and Katie's eyes widened.

'It's a gas cooker!' It was one of the very latest models, she had seen them in the window of a large store near where her brother lived, and longed to try one out, and now here was one within touching distance, resplendent with all the latest gadgets.

'Mrs Morris had it fitted in last year, miss. Your grandfather liked his food,' Amy told her. 'He was a very particular man about his meals, though he didn't eat enough to bait a mouse. Now my Ben, he's got a wonderful appetitie,' she beamed.

'Has it gone wrong?' Katie was not prepared to discuss Ben's appetite; on the subject of food she shared her grandfather's discriminating standards, and felt she was on delicate ground here with Amy. 'This doesn't seem to work.' She turned one of the taps experimentally, but there was no rewarding hiss of gas. 'I'll have to get someone in to see

47

to it . . .'

'Oh, it works all right, miss,' Amy hastened to assure her. 'It's me as doesn't get on with it.' She regarded the shiny new cooker more in sorrow than in anger. 'You has to light pilot lights and things,' she explained vaguely, 'and I was forever forgetting to put a match to the one in the oven, then when I came to light it the thing'd go bang and I'd drop the dishes.' Katie remembered the crash before breakfast and reckoned the gas was not the only reason for the chipped dishes she had seen. Amy seemed a born butterfingers. 'Ben cut the gas off here in the corner,' Amy indicated a master tap further along the floor, 'he said I'd blow the place up, else, and I went back to using the grate,' she finished thankfully.

'You must be very busy with the housework and all—and I've come and made you extra.' Katie looked suitably concerned. Amy had unintentionally paved the way for her.

'Oh, you'll be no trouble, miss. Like I said, I'm right glad you've come.' Katie felt a warm feeling grow inside her; it was good to know someone in the household was glad she had come. Even Ben had looked at her dourly, reserving judgment, she guessed. 'But I do find the cooking a bit much,' her companion confessed. 'It keeps me from doing the house as I like it.' She gave a

48

discontented glance about her spotless workplace.

'Maybe I could help? I'm not much good at housework, I'm afraid,' Katie added hastily, 'but I can manage some reasonable cooking,' she understated hopefully.

'*You* can, miss?' Her companion's surprise was unflatteringly like that which Ross had shown, and stemmed from the same source, Katie suspected. 'I thought you was an artist, I heard Mr Bailey tell Mr Ross...'

'Even artists have to learn to cook.' Katie ruthlessly destroyed another innocent illusion. 'And I must have some occupation while I'm waiting for my brother and his family,' she pressed her case, and was rewarded by an easy victory.

'I'll show you where the saucepans and things are kept,' Amy said hastily. She evidently did not intend to give her rescuer time to change her mind, and for the next half hour she and Katie were immersed in the mysteries of store cupboards and pantry shelf stocks that, from their sophistication, branded the departed housekeeper as an experienced cook of considerable prowess, though Katie suspected that to Amy they still remained a mystery.

'That sounds like Mr Ross now.' Men's voices could be heard through the opening door of the dining room. 'I'll go and clear the table, then I can start on these things.' Amy looked towards the stacked sink, and fumbled for a tray that leaned against the back of the old-fashioned dresser. She pulled open the kitchen door and the voice of her husband, anything but inarticulate now in the presence of another man, came clearly through the opening, a stubborn note of anger raising it several degrees over its normal tone.

'It's no good agoin' on, gaffer,' Ben said firmly in response to a comment from Ross. Katie could not hear what the comment was, he was still too far inside the dining room for his actual words to be audible. 'I'll tell tha' now to tha' face, I ain't takin' orders from no 'ooman!'

CHAPTER THREE

'My man's a bit old-fashioned,' remarked Amy placidly, preparing to sally forth with her tray. 'Now, Ben, out of my way, I want to get about the washing up.' She moved her spouse from his stance by the door, and Ross too, thought Katie with a quick flash of amusement, watching her disappear inside the dining room with a purposeful air.

Katie stood undecided for a moment, not quite knowing whether to smile at Ben or not, but he made the decision for her. With an odd little salute, and a nod like Jeremy

Bailey, he passed by her and made his way out of doors; then she heard the kitchen door slam behind him in a decided fashion as if his feelings still ran high.

That's four people I've run foul of up to now, thought Katie ruefully. Jeremy Bailey—he had been kind, helpful even, but immovable in his decision to leave Ross in charge. Eve frankly resented her presence; she had not said so in so many words, she did not need to, for one look from her green eyes had been quite enough. Ross had been the dutiful host last night, and pleasant enough at breakfast time this morning, but he must think her a nuisance, Katie thought bitterly. She was a guest in a house where no one had time for her, which was probably why he had suggested bringing her a dog 'to keep you company', something that he had neither the time nor the inclination to do himself. And now her innocent request to Ben had ended in this ... Her spirits dropped lower as the catalogue lengthened.

'Have you looked round the house, yet?' Ross stood in the dining room doorway, watching her, Katie realised with a start, with that penetrating look in his blue eyes that had been there when they had been introduced, the day before. 'I'm just going into the study if you'd like to come?' he invited casually, and turned towards a door further along the hall, leaving the decision with her, rather as if

51

he didn't care whether she came or not, she thought hotly, rubbed raw by Ben's unjust response to her polite request, which Ross had asked her to make in the first place, she thought vexedly, aware that her morning was suddenly going wrong.

'Are you coming in?'

She became aware, too, that Ross was standing in the doorway along the hall, politely holding it open for her, and she checked her thoughts sharply, reminding herself of the necessity to stay on good terms with the members of the household, at least, for Mark's and Wyn's sake. She excluded Eve from the catalogue; it was unlikely that she and the other girl would hit it off under any circumstances, inside the house or out, she thought with a philosophic shrug that realised no one person could get along with the rest of the world without exception. If your wavelengths crossed, she reasoned, it should still be possible to behave in a civilised fashion, and at least avoid an open clash.

'This is—was—?' She stopped uncertainly.

'Your grandfather's study,' Ross finished for her. 'I've got to attend to a couple of bills that came this morning,' he waved two envelopes in his right hand, 'and I thought you might like—company.' He, too, hesitated and stopped, and Katie stared at him. How had he guessed what she was feeling? She had hardly known what her feelings were, herself.

Certainly she had not analysed them, except that she shrank from entering this one, especially personal, room in the house that her grandfather must have kept as his own. Or did Ross want to be there himself when she came in here? she wondered, watching him as he went naturally to the desk, sitting where her grandfather must have sat daily, drawing the top down and reaching for writing materials with an air of absorption in his task that tactfully gave her the privacy to roam around the room and examine it as she wished, while yet giving her a sense of his awareness of her presence, so that if she spoke to him she knew he would answer immediately. Did he want to emphasise, without actually saying so in words, that he was in charge of Mallets until her brother arrived to claim his own, and not she, whom her brother had sent specifically for that purpose? She bit her lip vexedly, and remembered something else.

'Was there any post for me?' Her irritation flared again at the indignity of being in a position that forced her to ask for her post, like a child, instead of receiving the household post as was her right, and doing the distributing herself.

'No, only these two bills. If there had been, I should have brought it to you right away,' Ross replied, without a pause in what he was writing. The slight sound of the pen

53

scratching across the surface of the paper was like the buzz of a bluebottle trapped inside a window pane, and she moved to the other side of the room to be rid of it, finding it a rasp to her already jangled nerves. She focused her mind on the pictures, seeking a diversion to calm her, and surprisingly finding one. The picture she was staring at, when her eyes took in what she looked at, instead of focusing inwards on her own anger, was of the same quality as the one in the dining room, and pleasurable surprise made her annoyance vanish.

'There are some good pictures here.' She spoke abstractedly. The one in front of her was first class, and she paid homage to the unknown artist.

'Your grandfather enjoyed paintings, he bought several to my knowledge,' Ross answered her. 'There's—another—over there.' Again there was an odd hesitation in his voice, and this time he glanced up at her, briefly, once more leaving the choice to her, and again Katie followed his suggestion and walked across the room, near to where he sat, but no longer writing. He leaned back in the chair watching her with a look that she might have thought sympathetic if she had noticed it, but she passed by him with her eyes scanning the wall for the hanging that she sought. It was in shadow when she found it, and she stepped to one side and pushed the curtain away so that the clear morning light fell across it, outlining the warm, smiling beauty of the woman portrayed there, sensitively depicted by the artist, who had put her initials 'K.K.' in the bottom right-hand corner.

'You're very like your mother.' He spoke gently, coming up behind her and placing steadying hands, one on each of her shoulders. 'K.K.,' he murmured, reading aloud the initials that must have been familiar to him. 'It's one of your paintings,' he stated the obvious, increasing the pressure on her shoulders as he heard her sharp intake of breath, and felt the slight tremor run through her slender frame.

'I always wondered where the painting had gone.' She spoke in a low, controlled voice. 'It was bought by mistake from one of my exhibitions. It was not meant to be sold, and I was never able to trace it afterwards. Fortunately, I was able to paint another...'

'And now it belongs to Mark.' His calm statement steadied her, and she turned to face him.

'Is this,' she gestured towards the painting, 'why you thought I might want company when I came in here?'

'For the first time? Yes,' he admitted. 'I thought coming face to face with one of your own paintings—this particular painting—might be a shock for you,' he said quietly.

'Are there any more shocks in store for me?' Her voice was sternly controlled, and she held her chin high, a defiant gesture that brought a gleam to the man's eyes that could have been admiration.

'Not of this kind.' His tone was gentle. 'The rest of the house is more or less the same as the rooms you've already seen. Come with me, and I'll show you.'

He paused beside the desk to slide the top shut, touching the two envelope flaps with his tongue, and running a brown finger along the edges to seal them firmly. 'If you've got any letters for posting, leave them on the hall table,' he dropped his own there as they passed, 'whoever goes into the village automatically picks them up and takes them to the post office. And, of course, if you go into the village at any time, it would be a help if you'd do the same.' It wasn't quite an instruction, thought Katie, but his manner said he expected her to conform which left her undecided whether to feel pleased that he had included her in the routine of the rest of the household, or resentful that he expected her to obey his orders.

Oh, stop it! she told herself. Every time Ross speaks you start analysing what he's said and how he's said it. She couldn't go on like this, she decided, and summoning up politeness which, in a way, she thought, served well enough until you decided whether you liked a person or not, she smiled acquiescence.

'Of course I will.' Was her voice just a shade over-enthusiastic? 'I haven't been into Little Twickenham yet. I only passed through it on the way to the solicitor's office yesterday, but it looked worth exploring. It didn't look all that little, either,' she commented, finding the politeness easier as she went along.

'It's a biggish village,' Ross agreed amiably. Was he, too, using politeness to make up for a friendliness that he didn't feel? The thought rubbed a little, Katie found, though there was no reason why it should, since it merely reflected her own attitude to him. 'And if you like old places, you'll enjoy prodding round the odd corners.' It was odd that he should use that expression, she thought, it was one she herself found handy. She had enjoyed 'prodding round odd corners' in quite a few countries, and discovered a lot of interesting facts, and friends, while she was about it. 'Little Twickenham acts as the market village for the surrounding hamlets,' he explained. 'In fact, I'll be going in myself tomorrow, to the market,' he remembered. 'If you'd like to come along you'll be welcome.'

'Are you going to sell the bull?' Katie looked up at him hopefully, and a grin split his firm lips.

'No, I'm not. If your brother's interested in

farming, and from what I've heard he is, he'd never forgive me,' he retorted. 'I'm after a billygoat,' he enlarged.

'Oh, my goodness!' Katie groaned. 'Can't you get something that isn't savage?' she begged him. 'First that gander, then the bull. Oh, I know you said he's harmless,' she checked his swift retort, 'but I can't say I'm keen to find out. Now a pet lamb might be nice, they're gentle,' she smiled coaxingly.

'It's because the lambs are so gentle that I want a goat,' Ross replied grimly. 'A big, savage billy,' he said hopefully, then noticing her expression he put a comforting hand on her shoulder. 'Not to frighten you,' he assured her. 'I want it to frighten dogs. We're having a bit of sheep worrying, and I want to nip it in the bud before any harm comes of it,' he explained. 'It's not much, really. Just that in the spring people come for a run in the country, and they let their dogs loose in the fields. They don't realise the damage panic can do among a flock, and your grandfather's got a very nice one,' he said appreciatively. 'Small, but well bred, and firm, sturdy sheep that make good lambers. I'd like him to have a good yield this year,' he added half to himself, and Katie glanced at him quickly. There was one side of Ross she liked, she realised. He evidently took his stewardship seriously, and not only for the advantage it was to him. Jeremy Bailey had intimated that they were doing one another a good turn, but because of his friendship for her grandfather. And he had a sense of responsibility to Mark as well, she realised. His response when she suggested he sold the bull made that plain enough.

'How will a billygoat help in a flock of sheep?' She was puzzled by his reasoning. 'Mark keeps goats, and he had a pet ewe once as well, but they never made friends,' she remembered.

'I don't want him to make friends with the sheep, I just want him to hate all dogs,' Ross laughed. 'You'll see, when we've got him.' He automatically included her in the search, which mollified her feelings somewhat as she trekked dutifully after him through one room after another of the extensive house. 'That's the lot,' he paused at the head of the stairs, 'except for my bedroom and yours,' he added, and waited.

'We'll skip those,' Katie decided. She would have liked to see Ross's bedroom. It was the second of the guest bedrooms, and must have had a nice view from the windows, but it would look like prying, and she shrank from that.

'There's only the attics, then,' Ross inclined his head towards the flight of stairs, narrower and uncarpeted, that rose above them to the very top storey.

'I'll save those for a rainy day.' Katie had a

conscience about wasting too much of his time. He must have his own land to look after as well, and something told her that he was looking after Mallets without payment, which was a point she could not question him about. He was not the sort of person to whom you could put such a query, she thought, giving a wary glance at the rather uncompromising jawline that she had to tilt her head back to see. Ross must be well over six feet, she judged, uncricking her neck. Nevertheless it put herself, and Mark, under no obligation to him, which was a position she personally would have preferred not to be in, although the arrangement was not of her doing.

'In that case I'll get off.' He did not say where to, or what he intended to do, and Katie let him go, her mind already intent on what she would cook for lunch. The extensive range which the pantry and store cupboard offered was a temptation in itself to anyone who liked cooking, and it was a hobby that she enjoyed and had never had much opportunity to indulge. Maybe she could even wean Ben off 'good plain stuff', she thought with a smile, and perhaps teach Amy how to use the gas stove, as well as coax her to raise her sights even slightly above the ill done meat and two veg which she had swallowed under protest the evening before. She regarded the large joint of beef, of which there was a goodly quantity left over. She shuddered as she thought of swallowing it at dinner last night. The thought of it sliced up cold was equally unappetising, but it would make nice beef cutlets, she thought; it would give it the extra flavour it required without spoiling it.

She sorted out the mincing machine and got busy, completely absorbed in her task. Soon she had the butter melted and the shaped cutlets bound by egg yolk and heating gently in the frying pan, round which she had rubbed a piece of garlic clove. She had hesitated over the garlic. Not everyone liked the flavour, however slight, but she decided that the departed Mrs Morris would not have hesitated, so she went ahead. A bubble of distress from a saucepan told her the shallots had boiled for long enough, and soon they, too, were browning nicely in buttery fat while she halved a generous dishful of tomatoes and popped them under the grill with the bacon which Amy cut for her from a side hung in the cold store. Grating the horseradish made her eyes water, but she persevered, enjoying her task, and finishing it off with a Spanish sauce that she had learned to enjoy while she had been in that country working during the previous year. A search of the spices unearthed chilli peppers and tomato puree, and to her delight some good cider vinegar, and Amy supplied her with a jug of cream.

By the time she had chopped the parsley

she felt hungry herself, and justifiably proud of the two long serving dishes generously filled with the repast fit for any gourmet, with a bowl of sauce for each table, one for Amy and Ben, whom Katie could see making his way towards the kitchen and his lunch, and one for herself and Ross in the dining room. The egg whites left over from the cutlets she whipped into a quick meringue, which she instructed Amy to remove from the oven when the kitchen clock struck the half hour, which it would do by the time they had all finished their first course, she judged. She glanced up as Ben clumped into the scullery next door and began to sluice himself clean under the tap in preparation for his meal.

'Where's Ross?' She could not see the other man behind him. 'Maybe he's gone in the other way,' she added. Perhaps he'd come in the front door and made straight for the cloakroom to clean up the same as Ben.

'Isn't Mr Ross with you, Ben?' Amy shouted through the scullery door. 'Where's he got to? His dinner's ready.' She clucked her tongue with the frustration of having good food go cold.

'I'll serve ours here,' Katie decided, 'and leave his in the oven for a few minutes, it's shame to let it spoil.' She suited action to her words, keeping one oven glove on to carry her own plate into the dining room that Amy had already prepared. The plate was piping hot and she did not want her fingers scorched. She heard Ben clatter across the quarry floor of the kitchen as he finished his ablutions and made for the table, and his voice raised in astonished query as he regarded the results of her culinary efforts.

'What's this?' He did not sound too enthusiastic, thought Katie, and waited.

'It's Spanish beef.' Amy sounded proudly knowledgeable, and Katie smiled. 'Miss Katie made it.'

'Well, she can eat it, then,' Ben replied sourly. 'I want some of that cold beef, like we always has the day after a roast. We always has cold meat and mashed,' he repeated plaintively, 'an' some pickle to go with it...'

Katie shut the door behind her hastily, and made for the dining room. If Ben didn't like it, Ross would, she assured herself, tackling her own with relish. The sauce, piquantly flavoured, turned the cutlets into a feast, but it was one she seemed destined to enjoy alone, she thought, her annoyance mounting as the minutes ticked by and still Ross did not appear for the meal she had taken such a lot of trouble to prepare. Her eyes stung, suddenly, and she reached for her glass of water. I've overdone the peppers in the sauce, she told herself, dabbing at her eyes with her handkerchief, refusing to admit that fury over scorned meal was partly responsible for her blurred sight. She pocketed her lace-edged square of lawn hastily as a thud on the door preceded Amy's arrival with the sweet. She put it down on the table and a sudden thought struck Katie. 'Where's Mr Heseltine?' she asked Amy. Surely he hadn't remained in the kitchen with the others. That really would be too much.

'Ben says he's gone down to see Miss Clements—her as runs the riding school,' Amy replied shortly, clearing away the used plates and substituting the sweet. 'I dunno when he'll be back, neither.' From her tone her temper was frayed, and Katie looked up at her searchingly.

'The meringue is for all of us, not just Mr Heseltine and me,' she pointed out, cutting her own, and spooning it on to her dish.

'I'll take mine, miss, and keep the rest for Mr Ross when—if—he comes back.' Amy's lips were a sharp line of temper, and she hesitated, obviously wanting to say something else, but not sure whether she should.

'Yes?' Katie encouraged her.

'Well, I likes your Spanish beef, miss, if there's others who don't,' Amy burst out, unable to control her feelings any longer. 'An' as for the pudden,' she gestured towards Katie's fluffy meringue, 'I'm havin' some of that too, an' Ben, he can have the cold rice left over from yesterday.' She swept the dish on to the tray with an angry gesture that made Katie shudder for the contents, and flounced out of the room. Her footsteps could be heard clattering along the hall, ending in a thud that told Katie she had put her foot against the door to push it open, a habit that left a kick mark a few inches up every door she entered. It was a good job she wore soft shoes, Katie thought, digging her spoon into her 'pudden' without relish.

Ross had not said he would be away for lunch. If he had gone to see Eve no doubt she had invited him to stay, and no doubt he had accepted gladly. The prospect of escaping Amy's cold meat and mashed would be enough to tempt anyone to lunch out, thought Katie, struggling to be fair. She hadn't told Ross she would be cooking the lunch herself, though he knew she was intending to take over the meals from now on, and it was inconsiderate of him not to let her know that he would be out. Maybe it was not only the thought of a civilised meal that had tempted him to remain away, either, she thought, remembering Eve had called him 'darling', implying a relationship which must exist, since he had done nothing to deny it. She pushed her sweet away only half eaten, her appetite gone, and reached for her coffee.

'What shall I do with the other dinner, miss?' Amy wanted to know when she came to clear away the dishes.

'Put it in the pig swill,' Katie retorted, then grinned, her good humour, which never deserted her for long, slowly seeping back. 'I shouldn't put the sauce in with it, though, the pigs might find the peppers a bit hot,' she advised. 'I'll do something a bit more conservative for dinner,' she promised. 'We can't have Ben leaving his meals,' she added drily.

'He made up with bread and cheese,' his wife admitted, 'but I enjoyed it,' she said wistfully. 'It isn't often I have a meal cooked for me.'

Few married women did, reflected Katie, seeking the sunshine and a walk to allow her own lunch to go down. She hesitated at the white wicket gate in the garden wall, but Ben was busy pumping water at the well in the middle of the yard. She did not particularly wish to encounter the hand after his declaration that he did not intend to take orders from a 'ooman' and his subsequent refusal of her good food. She was unsure of his response if she spoke to him in the yard, so she turned the other way, out of the garden and into the fields that were bright gold with buttercups, staining her shoes with pollen. Buttercups ... Apprehensively her eyes scanned her surroundings, but there was no sign of the bull. A small flock of sheep grazed placidly a couple of fields away, their growing lambs energetic beside them, but there seemed nothing between herself and the stream. The Burley Brook, Ross had called it.

It was a nice name for a watercourse. It was a nice brook, she thought, running her fingers in the coolness of it, stooping low to examine the minute white water flower that carpeted it in deceptively solid-looking rafts here and there, hiding the tiny minnow that streaked for shelter as she splashed.

She rose to her feet, and walked along beside it, unconsciously soothed by its muted chatter, and reluctant to leave its company. The spring grass was soft under her feet, the turf springy with close proximity to the water. Buttercups gave way to ladysmocks and cowslips, that relished the dampness, and responded by an abundance of delicate bloom that made her linger just to be among them. She'd pick a few for her room on the way back, she decided, resisting the temptation now for fear her posy might wilt if she remained out for long. She paused beside a plank that strode the water to the other side. Ross said she could walk on the Lodge land if she wished, but the means of access looked precarious, to say the least.

'It's come adrift from its moorings. Let me make it safe for you.' Ross's voice sounded from just behind her, and she spun round, startled.

'I didn't hear you ...' she began, annoyed that he should walk up on her unawares. He obviously thought it was amusing that he had made her jump, she thought crossly, seeing a smile across his face.

'I should have called out,' he acknowledged, bending to lift the plank and set it firmly on a square of bricks roughly stacked in the rushes about a foot away. 'The trouble was,' he squinted along the plank, intent on lining it up with a similar stack of bricks on the other side of the brook, 'I was so intent on catching you up I didn't think to cooee. Let go, Glen!' as the tall, chocolate-coloured dog padded up to investigate, and splashed water happily in all directions.

'He's only trying to help,' Katie gurgled, laughter dimpling her cheeks as the man ducked out of the way of the spray.

'Well, he's not succeeding,' Ross wiped himself dry ruefully. 'The youngsters from the riding school move the plank now and then, they like it to wobble a bit when they run across, it's more fun.'

'For them, maybe.' Katie stepped on it gingerly, then finding it firm under her feet she went forward with more confidence.

'Hold on to me.' Ross came behind her and caught at her outstretched hands, steadying her as the stream got deeper in the middle, and lapped against the sides of the plank that bent with their joint weight in a fashion that Katie found disconcerting. Glen splashed beside them through the water, having to resort to swimming for a few feet until the bank shelved upwards again on the other side.

'He doesn't mind getting wet.'

'He swims at every opportunity,' responded Ross. 'Look out!' He grabbed her and swung her behind him hastily as the dog shook its thick coat dry, regardless of the proximity of the two humans. 'He's not above giving you a shower bath,' he said— unnecessarily, thought Katie, remembering suddenly that she was annoyed with her companion for missing lunch, and stiffening in his arms, so that he gave her a surprised look and removed them from about her, but not before he made certain she was sure-footed on the level ground beyond the edge of the bank.

'You didn't say you'd be out for lunch,' Katie accused him. She might as well thrash the matter out with him now, she decided. If she was taking over the cooking, the least he could do was to be punctual for meals, or let her know if he intended to be out. Common courtesy dictated that, if nothing else, she thought crossly, ignoring the small inner voice of her own innate fairness that told her it was not in Ross's nature to be discourteous.

What do you know about his nature? she squashed the voice cruelly. You haven't known the man five minutes. And anyhow, Amy had said he'd been to see Eve. Love evidently made people forgetful, as well as blind, she thought scathingly, and the small voice of fairness inside her lapsed into silence, defeated by her stubborn refusal to listen.

'I didn't think you'd be cooking lunch,' he responded mildly, turning beside her automatically along the watercourse, and reaching out a cautioning arm to steer her round a clump of rushes that cloaked a crumbling piece of bank. 'Mind how you step, here,' he warned her, 'it's treacherous,' and absent mindedly left his hand under her elbow, so that they walked closely together while Glen cast about ahead of them, released for the moment from his usual position at his master's heels. 'Something cropped up,' he did not say what, 'and I had to take the opportunity while it was there. It was too good to miss.' He left his sentence in mid-air, tantalisingly, and Katie looked up at him quickly. It was on the tip of her tongue to ask him if he'd bought the goat he wanted, and then her eyes met his smile and she tightened her lips determinedly.

I won't ask him what it was, she squashed her curiosity. If Eve had asked him to stay for lunch, that was his affair, not hers. Her eyes sparkled angrily as she visualised Eve's malicious pleasure if she ever became aware that she had succeeded in ruining the lunch, and determined that the other girl should not know of it if she, Katie, could possibly help it. Ross might tell her, of course. Might laugh about it with her, if he thought it had annoyed Katie...'

'It didn't matter,' she told him indifferently, 'it's just that I don't like waste. It can go in the pig swill,' implying by her tone that she was just as happy if the pigs instead of her companion ate what she had prepared.

'Ouch!' Ross looked down at her, his smile vanished. 'For your size you hit hard,' he conceded, and Katie flushed, half repenting her sharpness. It had verged on rudeness, she told herself guiltily, and it was not like her to be rude. No matter what her own feelings were, she must—repeat *must*—remember that this man would eventually be her brother's neighbour, and she would do well to keep on the right side of him if only for appearances' sake. People reacted to people quite differently, she told herself, and however unlikely it seemed to her, it could be that Mark and Wyn might even like the man. She tilted her head back and met his eyes without flinching.

'It's time I started back, or there won't be enough of the afternoon left to cook the dinner in,' she told him firmly. 'And I want that ready by seven o'clock.' She paused, giving him the opportunity to say he would not be in, but he inclined his head for her to go on. 'I don't want a repeat of last night's joint,' she finished with a shudder.

71

'You ate it nobly.' His smile was back, his voice teasing, and with an effort she responded, remembering her vow regarding Mark and Wyn.

'Nevertheless, I don't want another ill-cooked joint.' She paused, but his hand on her elbow pressed her forward.

'Walk just a few yards more, I'd got to come this way anyhow, and it'll save me another journey if we go on a little further, just to the other side of that gate.' He pointed ahead to where a gate led into what was evidently a boundary fence of some kind.

'Very well, another half hour won't hurt,' she gave in, and wondered what would have brought him this way. Perhaps it was the way to Eve's house? Although she gathered the impression that the girl had turned in the opposite direction along the lane when she left the house the previous evening, going towards where the village lay, not away from it. If Eve did live beyond where the fence lay—it was lined deeply with shrubs so that she could not see beyond them—she did not particularly wish to encounter her again, but she could think of no reasonable excuse for remaining behind, and each stride he took with his long legs, she had to step out smartly to keep up with him, brought the gate closer to them. He swung it open, courteously waiting for her to go through, and making sure Glen preceded them before shutting it carefully behind them, and rapping the latch down hard with the flat of his hand to be sure it stayed shut. A large clump of holly bushes restricted their view, and he steered her round them, following the dog that had already gone on ahead, evidently sure of the way.

'Oh!' Katie paused as the view cleared ahead of them. 'Oh, what a shame,' she added as they came closer to the cluster of buildings that lay ahead of them, and she saw that what had looked like solid thatch from behind, now revealed itself as only half a roof as they veered to one side round another clump of shrubs and approached it from a slightly different direction. The house, of the same warm-coloured stone as Mallets, but built in an octagonal shape, which gave it a fairytale attraction, looked for all the world like a cottage loaf with its crust torn off. Bared spars of wood lay open to the skies, revealing rooms of surprising size, and as they approached a man descended from a ladder propped against a wall and came towards them.

''Art'noon, Mr Heseltine. Miss,' he nodded towards Katie, including her in his greeting. 'It's coming on nicely,' he told Ross.

'Off, you mean,' Ross retorted ruefully. 'How long do you think it'll be before...'

'We'll have the old thatch cleared from the

73

house and the new spars up by the end of the week if the weather holds.' The man cast an appraising eye at his work of destruction, which looking at the charred roof timbers, and the scorched appearance of some of the old thatch that lay in a heap on the floor not far from the ladder, was not all of his doing, Katie surmised. She let her eyes roam over the near-roofless house, gleaning information that sent her cold with realisation of what must have happened there.

'There's been a bad fire,' she deduced. 'And under thatch, too ...' Her vivid imagination filled her eyes with horror, and something clicked in her mind. A memory as teasing as Ross's eyes when he had looked down at her earlier, as they walked along the bank of the stream. She looked up at him, seeing his dark head outlined against the bright sky, the brown skin of his face sharply marked by the pallor of the scar that touched his temple. The scar made by a burn.

'Yes, there's been a fire,' he confirmed, and now his eyes were brooding, their blue darkened into near black as they looked through narrowed lids at the scene in front of them, the horror in them caused by memory and not by imagination. 'This is the Lodge,' he said quietly. 'My home—or what's left of it.'

CHAPTER FOUR

'He was lucky to escape with his life,' Amy gossiped happily as she peeled apples beside Katie at the kitchen table. She did not enjoy cooking, but she volunteered to help with the chores such as peeling and scraping, and, to Katie's relief, washing up. She was flatteringly glad of another woman's company, and now she had lost her initial wariness, chattered happily whenever they were together.

'How did it start?' Katie asked. Sensitive to others' feelings, she would not ask Ross himself, and they had strolled back to Mallets in near silence, broken only when he stooped to help her pick a posy before they left the banks of the stream, both of them glad of the distraction of trivialities to come between themselves and their thoughts.

'Some children lit a fire, and didn't put it out properly,' Amy explained. 'The wind got up in the night and blew the sparks on to the roof of the Lodge. We'd had a good month of dry weather, particularly wind, and it went up like tinder.'

'So that's how Ross—Mr Heseltine—got that awful scar.'

'That's right,' Amy nodded confirmation. 'It was his dog woke him up by howling the

75

place down. He could have got out himself without any trouble, but his housekeeper panicked and wouldn't come down the stairs or out of the window, so Mr Ross went back in after her. He got her out all right, and himself by the skin of his teeth just as the roof collapsed. One of the wooden spars hit him as it came down, that's what the scar is,' she said gloomily. 'Spoiled his looks, it has, an' he'll carry it till the day he dies,' she added with gloomy relish.

'Well, they're making a good job of stripping the old thatch. The man we saw told us it would be done by the end of the week if the weather holds,' Katie imparted her news, determined to be cheerful. 'And the Lodge looks as if it could be a nice house when it's got a roof on. It's a bit like a cottage loaf,' she said, remembering its shape.

'It's fair enough, in its way,' replied Amy grudgingly, determined not to be diverted. 'But it isn't a patch on the old Manor.'

'What's that?' Katie was intrigued. She knew nothing about Ross, except that he was a neighbour and friend of her grandfather's, and now, of course, she knew the reason why he was glad of accommodation at Mallets while he kept his eye on the farm; he would be homeless otherwise unless he camped out in one of the downstairs rooms of his own house, which Katie acknowledged would be less than comfortable under the circumstances.

'Why, he belongs to Heseltine Manor, miss.' Amy looked at her, surprised. 'Only when his father died, he sold the place. It's a country club now. Couldn't keep it up, see, what with death duties and all,' she said, her gloom deepening. 'Don't seem right, somehow, him living at the Lodge.'

'It looks a big enough place,' Katie remembered. 'The rooms that were uncovered on the top storey were big ones.' They had been huge by modern standards, but probably in comparison with a manor house they looked small enough to Amy.

'Oh, it's big enough,' Amy cheered up a little, 'it was the dower house, see? Not just coachman's quarters, nor anything like that, it was built for a member of the family to live in, so they made it generous, like.'

I wonder if he misses it? Katie watched him covertly over the dinner table, at which he had presented himself on the dot of seven o'clock, to Katie's annoyance, since the roast needed another ten minutes to make it really palatable, and his raised eyebrows and quizzical look accused the cook herself of not turning up on time on this occasion. He did not say so in so many words, which vexed her even more, since she could have retaliated if he had spoken, and now she was condemned to silence by his own self-restraint.

'I cooked something plain, for Ben's sake,'

Katie gave him an opening, but he seemed determined to be amiable, which ought to shame her into the same behaviour, her conscience told her.

'Ben deserves bread and water if he doesn't enjoy this,' her companion commented callously, tucking into the new lamb and peas, and young potatoes, garnished with tiny, button mushrooms, and minted with leaves fresh from the garden, with an enjoyment that could only have been genuine.

'Ben's eaten his dinner,' Amy confirmed, coming in to clear away the plates, and hearing what Ross said. 'My, but it was nice,' she said appreciatively. 'And he's partial to apple pie, so he'll eat his pudden, too.' She put down the serving dish and plates beside Katie—almost as if we're married, she thought with sudden amusement, and looked up at Ross.

'Shall I serve you?' she said meekly, and for a moment his eyes sparked, but conscious of Amy's presence in the room he forbore to comment, merely inclining his head with a courteous 'Thank you.' 'Help yourself to cream.' Katie passed him his dish and the jug, and started on her own, choosing soft brown sugar in place of the cream. 'It's nice to be idle.' She stretched out her legs towards the small fire and reached for her coffee after the meal had been cleared away, and they had both drifted towards the drawing room on hearing the clink of cups. 'Don't let me detain you, if you have anything to do,' she said politely, noticing that Ross were listening to every noise that penetrated through the open window. Not that many did; it was a peaceful spot to live, thought Katie, grateful for the quiet, but her companion seemed—not ill at ease, but as if he was waiting for something—or someone? Maybe Eve was coming up, or . . . Footsteps sounded outside the door, and Ross rose swiftly to his feet, as if he had been expecting them. They were a man's footsteps—Ben's, she realised, as the farmhand's head appeared through the door in answer to Ross's called 'come in'.

'The carrier brought un down, gaffer. Said he thought to save tha' a journey,' Ben's broad voice told Ross. The wolds bred a dialect that even after such a short time Katie found she was getting used to, and rather liked, the sound of it was akin to the colour of the stone that made the dwellings, warm sounding, and in any other circumstances, welcoming, she thought. She didn't feel welcome with anyone but Amy, but that was another matter . . . Ross's voice was only slightly tinged with the homely burr, just enough to richen it, though Katie had noticed when he spoke to Ben, if he wanted to emphasise a point he relapsed into the vernacular in a way that sat oddly on him, but which he must have found effective since it was obvious the destruction of his native language did not come naturally to his normally cultured speech.

'That was kind of him,' Ross responded. 'He said he might, if he was coming this way, and it's certainly saved me from having to go out tonight. I didn't particularly want to.' That too sounded odd, thought Katie disparagingly, unless he expected Eve to come to him. Maybe he was just keeping up a show of reluctance in front of Ben and herself, she thought, turning away indifferently as Ross reached out and took something that the farmhand held out to him. She was determined not to show curiosity, if Ross wanted to keep her at arms' length about farm matters she would not give him the satisfaction of showing even mild interest, she vowed.

'Thanks, Ben.' The door shut behind the farmhand, and Ross turned back into the room. 'Don't step back, Katie,' he warned her, 'or you'll trip yourself up.'

A small, warm body pushed against her foot, scrabbling over her shoe in its eagerness to make itself known, and Katie looked down into two bright button eyes in a spiky halo of puppy fur.

'Oh! Aren't you sweet!' In an instant she was on her knees on the rug, her coffee forgotten, and both hands going out to clasp the wriggling white scrap with the three brown patches that tumbled over itself in its haste to be picked up. Ross reached out and carefully pushed her cup of coffee further on to the table.

'Now perhaps you'll forgive me for not coming in to lunch,' he said drily. 'I didn't hear of this particular litter until I was in the village this morning.' So he had gone to see Eve as Amy said, thought Katie, a momentary cloud marring the brightness of her eyes. 'It was no good waiting until they'd all been promised before I went along.'

'I'm sorry ...' Katie felt contrite, regretting her sharpness earlier, though if he'd explained it would have saved a lot of ill feeling, she thought, some of her impatience returning. It was all very well being strong and silent, but the silent bit could cause a lot of misunderstandings, so really it was as much his fault as hers.

'Not half as sorry as I was, when I found my lunch feeding the pigs,' retorted Ross grimly. 'I made do on bread and cheese, the same as Ben,' he told her with feeling, and she flushed guiltily.

'You could have phoned,' she reminded him, her chin coming up. She would not accept responsibility for his thoughtlessness, and if he lunched off bread and cheese it would teach him not to be so careless in future, she told herself, but she did not say so. A set of small teeth sharpening themselves

81

on the end of her thumb brought her attention rapidly back to the fourlegged delinquent in her arms. 'Let go, that hurts!' She pulled her thumb out of reach of a minute pair of jaws that snapped with a tiny click behind it.

'He's lively enough,' laughed Ross unsympathetically. 'Don't let him bite you,' he added, gently turning the tiny creature's head away from her hand. 'Start as you mean to go on, and make sure he does as he's told.'

'What sort is he?'

'He's a Jack Russell terrier, they're not very big,' Ross answered her. 'This one will only grow to about fourteen inches at the most, but if you let them know who's master—mistress,' he corrected himself with a smile, 'they make wonderful companions. They've got wills of their own, the Jack Russells,' he warned her, 'so don't stand any nonsense, however appealing he may look to you now.'

'It is a—a—he?' Katie went pink, but she had to know so that she could give the little animal a suitable name. She once had to change her kitten's name from Jon to Joan, and the embarrassment stayed with her still.

'It's a dog, never fear.' Ross's eyes twinkled at her confusion, with a merry glint in them that made her want to smack him, only she had both hands full of wriggling mischief that seemed intent on making a meal of her finger ends. 'I thought it best to be on the safe side, rather than risk your brother's wrath when he took over,' he told her with a gravity that his laughing eyes denied. So he, too, was being careful of future relationships, thought Katie; maybe that was why he was trying to be pleasant to her, so that he could start off on a good footing with her brother and his family when they eventually arrived. The thought galled her, although it was only her own policy in reverse, and her innate honesty acknowledged the sense of such an outlook.

'I thought tha'd like a basket for un, miss.' Ben reappeared at the door with a wickerwork skip in his hand, and surprisingly, a piece of pale blue blanket that looked out of its element in his sturdy grasp.

'Why, Ben, how kind . . . thank you,' Katie stammered, completely taken aback by the farmhand's thoughtfulness after his scowling disapproval of the day before. 'This is lovely and soft.' She fingered the piece of blanket he held out to her.

'Likely he'll tear it up,' the farmhand replied gruffly, ill at ease under Katie's gratitude, 'but it'll keep un warm meantime,' and he disappeared through the door again, avoiding her eye.

'Why so surprised?' Ross inquired mildly, taking the pup from her hands while she knelt on the hearth again and arranged the blanket in the bottom of the basket. 'Ben's a kindly man when you get to know him,' he chided gently.

'He didn't seem very kindly to me, yesterday,' Katie confessed ruefully. She had not meant to tell him, but there seemed no other way out, his eyes were too observant by half, she thought regretfully. 'I only asked him to come in and see you about the bags of feed, like you said, and I heard him snapping at you about not taking orders from an "ooman",' she mimicked the rich burr in a way that brought a grin to her companion's lips, 'as if I'd committed a crime. And all I did was pass on your message,' she finished unhappily. If only Mark had been able to come himself, it would have been a lot easier, she need never have met these people, she thought miserably, the blanket suddenly wavery before her eyes. 'It's not funny,' she snapped, looking up and meeting Ross's grin.

'It is when you realise it wasn't you Ben meant,' he laughed outright, and Katie's lips tightened, then parted as the implication of what he had said struck her.

'You mean...?'

'I mean it was Eve who had tried giving him orders. And come unstuck,' he chuckled. 'That's why I went down to see her at lunchtime, on my way to the village.' So it hadn't been a special journey, after all. Katie felt a twinge of remorse, but just the same he could have said ... 'She's a newcomer to the district,' he explained easily, 'and she isn't always careful about how she makes her wishes known. She tends to tell, rather than ask. It's just the way she's used to,' he said indulgently, 'but it doesn't always pay with the wold people, they need getting to know,' he said seriously.

'I thought she ran the riding school when Grandfather was alive. That hardly makes her a newcomer,' Katie pointed out. 'Amy implied she'd been here about two years.'

'Three,' corrected Ross, 'but according to the village folk she's still a newcomer,' he smiled.

'Poor Mark! And Wyn.' Katie felt sorry for her relatives if this was the case. Maybe the child might qualify to 'belong' by the time it was come of age, she thought waspishly, accustomed to a more open-minded outlook from her years of travelling, and finding this narrow parochialism difficult to understand.

'They won't be newcomers,' Ross assured her. 'They're family,' he pointed out.

'Their name isn't Spurr, it's Kimberley.'

'Their name makes no difference,' Ross responded. 'They belong to Mallets. That's enough!'

In that case, so did she, she thought, lying on her face in the pillows later on, with her one arm dangling over the edge of the bed in a manner that made it tingle with pins and needles to the elbow, but it allowed her fingers to reach into the wicker basket on the floor beside her, and rest on the bit of furry body that showed out of the blue blanket, which was the only way she had been able to quieten the pup short of taking it into her own bed, and that she was determined not to do. There were limits, and Ross had warned her that Jack Russells had got wills of their own. It had been difficult to resist the temptation, just the same, and only the thought of her brother's scorn when he would eventually take the young dog into his charge prevented her from cuddling it in her arms and allowing herself as well as the rest of the household to get some sleep, which they would not have been able to do, she guessed, if the little animal kept up its wails that proclaimed to the world its woe at sleeping for the first time on its own, without the rest of the litter around it.

It was good to know that Ben didn't disapprove of her completely, she thought, fingering the blanket. The farmhand's act of kindness had touched her more than she cared to admit, the feeling of being a nuisance when she had come all this way to be a help rubbed her friendly nature raw. It was only Eve and Ross who didn't want her now, she thought, and they didn't really matter. At least, Eve didn't. And Ross? She lay relaxed, listening drowsily to the sound of the wind bending the trees outside, and making the old house creak with the cooling air, as if it talked, as old houses did to the wind, whispering their secrets to the airy gusts that raised small puffs of dust on attic beams. She'd explore the attics another day, perhaps when it rained, but she'd do it alone, she thought drowsily, not with Ross. And she slid into sleep on the small wave of loneliness that the thought of exploring the rest of the house without him brought to her dreaming mind.

'Have you thought of a name for him yet?'

'I'm going to call him Quiz.' She turned back to the staircase as the puppy, unable to negotiate the steep steps on his too short legs, raised a yell of alarm. 'Come on, I'll carry you the rest of the way.' She tucked him under her arm, whereupon he began biting her thumb. 'So far he's investigated every nook and cranny in my bedroom, lost himself in the airing cupboard, and got tangled up in Amy's knitting bag,' she laughed. 'He's the most inquisitive creature I've ever come across.'

'Why not give your thumb a rest over breakfast?' Ross suggested drily. 'There's someone at the kitchen door who's willing to act as a temporary nursemaid. Her name's Emma,' he added, as she peered round the door, and lowered her sights to the level of the very small person dressed in Brownie's uniform who rocked backwards and forwards

87

on one foot on the edge of the step.

'Come further in or you'll fall.' Katie pulled the child from the edge hastily, and surveyed the thin freckled face under the brown woolly cap pulled down uncompromisingly over two fair plaits as tightly as her belt was pulled in over her uniform smock, making the skirt stick out sideways over the spindly legs.

'I'll look after him for you,' arms thin as the legs reached out and took Quiz from her, 'just while you have your breakfast,' the small girl offered gravely, and Katie relinquished the puppy with a smile.

'And who's Emma?' she asked Ross over her share of the boiled eggs.

'One of the children who comes up to the riding school for lessons,' Ross told her. 'She's one of the local doctor's brood. He's got three,' he said with some awe. 'Emma's the middle one, and she's very conscious of being a Brownie. This is her good deed for the day,' he said it in capital letters, and Katie smiled.

'In that case I wouldn't stop her,' she said generously, 'but I'd like him back afterwards, he's lovely company,' she smiled.

'I thought you were coming to the market with me, this morning?' His lips tightened slightly. 'You needn't·if you'd rather not, of course,' he added, and busied himself spooning sugar into his coffee.

'Of course I want to come.' She didn't, really. In fact she had forgotten that he had asked her, regarding it at the time as a politeness that he did not really mean, and nothing more. Now he had brought the subject up again she supposed she had better go, if only for the sake of appearances. 'I'd like to bring Quiz along as well, that's all.'

'Bring him by all means.' His lips resumed their normal easy line. 'You can fit him out with a halter and lead while you're about it,' he suggested. 'He's got to learn to walk to heel, and that's as easy a way as any of achieving it.' He pulled to a halt outside the corn chandler's in the village. 'We'd better get that halter and lead before we get to the market.' He eyed the pup with a mistrustful stare. 'I don't want him investigating the pens of animals, or there'll be uproar,' he paid rueful respect to the tiny dog's overweening sense of curiosity, that had got the whole household by their heels looking for him before they started out, finding him eventually in the boot cupboard, stuck fast inside one of Ben's big wellingtons, and guided to the rescue by his muffled howls of distress.

'I'd like the red one, he'll look smart in that.' Katie chose the miniature halter and lead. 'I'll pay,' she protested, as Ross dug in his pocket for the necessary cash.

'Allow me,' he said grimly. 'I regard it as a

89

form of insurance.' He helped her up the step of the Land Rover, and waited while a bevy of children on cycles decided which way they intended to go before he started the engine.

'One, two—there's only three holes in that stocks,' Katie counted them twice to make sure. 'That's odd, it doesn't look as if there's any of it missing.' The instrument of public punishment that sat in the middle of the village green looked sound enough, if ancient.

'There isn't,' Ross glanced briefly at the stocks. 'They cut the third hole to accommodate a reprobate with a wooden leg, they only needed to put his good one through the hole to hold him. I believe he was one of your ancestors,' he added maliciously, and grinned at Kate's suddenly furious glare. 'You can't help your ancestors,' he conceded loftily, 'so there's no need to look so upset.'

'I'm not upset,' she choked on her words, 'I just think it's a silly form of punisment. Barbaric,' she threw the word at him triumphantly. 'Oh, mind that delivery van!' as a baker's vehicle swung round the corner.

'He's going the other way.' Ross did not slacken speed, and Katie closed her eyes as the two vehicles rushed towards one another on what looked like a certain collision course.

'You can open them now.' Ross was openly amused, and her temper boiled over. 'He always does go the other way,' he added mildly.

'If he ever decides not to, I hope I'm not in the Land Rover with you at the time!' she flared, furious with herself for showing fear, and him for being the cause of it.

'You probably won't be,' he commented, unperturbed by her show of temper. 'I only come to the market about once a month. Haven't you got that pup into his halter yet?' He glanced down at her as he drew to a halt in the sale yard car park. 'Let me do it.' He applied the brake, and reached out to take the pup from her lap, putting an end to her fumbling with the buckle of the narrow halter straps that her suddenly trembling fingers found difficulty in doing up. 'There, that's fixed it. Now for the lead.' He clipped it to the halter ring and ran an exploratory finger round the body straps, making sure they were an easy fit and did not rub anywhere before he dropped the terrier back on to her knees. 'That'll check his exploring instincts, for the time being anyway,' he said with satisfaction. 'Though I should keep him in your arms while we're among the pens, or he'll need a bath before he's through,' he warned. 'And do stop him chewing your fingers!' His voice held a note of irritation.

'He's cutting his teeth,' Katie defended her new acquisition indignantly. 'All babies need to bite on something. You did, once,' she threw at him, and dimpled suddenly as she tried to imagine the large being beside her

91

reduced to infant size.

'Yes, but I didn't cut mine on my mother's fingers,' he retorted, his face reflecting her twinkle. 'A pup's teeth are sharp as needles, your fingers will be in rags by the time he's finished with them.' He took her hand in his and turned it upwards so that he could see her finger ends. 'Don't ruin these,' he commanded her. 'Your paintings give a lot of enjoyment to others, and you can't paint without fingers. Hold this and let him chew it,' he fished in his pocket and brought out a paper bag, from which he extracted a small, hard ball. 'I didn't intend him to have it until he got back home,' he confessed rather sheepishly at Katie's look of surprise, 'but it'll stop him reducing you to pulp. And ruining his new halter,' he fished the chest strap out of the pup's mouth and took up a bit more slack at the buckle. 'Now let's go and see if they've got a goat.' He took her arm determinedly, his attitude one that suggested he had wasted quite enough time already, and Katie trotted along beside him trying not to feel guilty. He had asked her to go, after all, it was his suggestion, not hers, but now she was here she found she was enjoying herself. A stock market was a novel experience to her, and she kept closely by his side, needing no urging to remain with him. There seemed an utter confusion of animals everywhere, some being unloaded from lorries and put into pens, while still others were being loaded up and taken away. 'This one looks as if he would do.'

'You're not buying—him?' Katie looked at the contents of the pen before her, aghast at the possibility.

'He looks ideal for my purpose.' Ross ignored her trepidation and glanced at the labelling on the pen.

'That un's a brute,' a broad voice told them with a laugh. 'You'll buy trouble if you buy un, mark my words,' and their adviser passed on his way with a cheery wave in Ross's direction.

'Just the same, I mean to try. He comes from Nixon of Barrow End,' he spoke as if he knew the present owner, thought Katie, 'so he's of good stock, and he'll be disease-free. Come on, it looks as if they're just going to start auctioning this lot. Our goat's been put among the miscellaneous sales,' he grinned, indicating a jumbled mixture of furniture and fittings topped by a large stuffed owl with a basilisk stare not unlike the goat, thought Katie, pulling a face at it as she passed by. 'It looks as if the owner might be glad to get rid of him, and be willing to take a reasonable price. Stand by me,' he instructed her, taking up a position close to the centre of the circle of people about the auctioneer, 'and stand still. It won't be for long.' He lapsed into silence as the man started his patter, and

Katie listened fascinated as one item after another was knocked down to eager buyers. The man's lung power seemed inexhaustible, he never ceased talking, and Katie marvelled at his vocal prowess as well as the speed of his delivery.

'There's Eve Clements,' she spoke quietly to Ross. 'On the other side of the crowd,' she guided his look. 'She's just bought some harness.' To her surprise Ross merely looked across at the girl and smiled, ignoring Eve's wave from behind the auctioneer's back. How bad-tempered, she thought, and raised her own hand in response. She did not particularly want to wave to the other girl, but they could not both of them ignore her greeting, she thought. Maybe Ross thought his smile was enough, the understanding between himself and Eve probably made it special, and Katie turned her attention back to the auctioneer, feeling she had done her duty, and hoping Eve would not join them on the way back.

'She can't,' Ross answered her query as the patter died down at last, 'we're taking the billy back with us. And you've got to go and collect that stuffed owl you bought,' he added with a grin. 'What on earth did you want that thing for? It's no good as a toy for Quiz,' he warned her, 'he'll choke on the feathers if you give him that.'

'What stuffed owl?' Katie remembered the

junk and odd bits of furniture piled beside the pens, even as she asked. 'I haven't bought any owl,' she denied firmly.

'You have,' his grin broadened. 'When you raised your hand just now, the auctioneer knocked it down to you. Quickly, before you changed your mind,' he dug. 'I'll bet he didn't think he'd get rid of that so easily.' His tone jibed and Katie flushed.

'I didn't raise my hand to him, I waved at Eve. Because you couldn't be bothered to,' she retorted sharply, stung by his laughter.

'Eve wouldn't expect me to raise my hand to her, not when I was facing an auctioneer,' he said simply. 'She knows better than to make movements like that at auctions. Whole estates have been knocked down to unsuspecting buyers at the movement of one eyebrow.' He made laughing capital out of her mistake.

So that was why Eve had waved. Katie choked on the thought. Eve knew she herself was well out of range of the auctioneer's line of vision, and she also knew that if Katie made a move it would be interpreted as a bid. She must have guessed her victim was ignorant of country sale yards, and she had taken spiteful advantage of that ignorance.

'Of all the things to do . . . !' She could get no further, and her face went scarlet with pent-up anger.

'It was your own fault. I did tell you to

stand still,' Ross reminded her, then capitulated as he put his hand round her waist to steer her in the direction of the yard office, and felt her rigid stance that betrayed her feelings even more plainly than her face, which in itself was eloquent enough. 'If you really don't want it I'll try and cancel the sale for you,' he offered, and Katie glanced up at him gratefully, then as she met the ill-concealed amusement that still lurked in his face her chin came up and the light of battle made her own look steely.

'I've got a use for it,' she told him shortly, remembering in time the small Brownie who had appeared on the kitchen doorstep at breakfast time, intent on doing her good deed for the day. 'I want it for—for—someone,' she said vaguely. She would not tell him who it was, she thought furiously, let him guess.

'We'll have to join the queue,' he indicated a small line of people outside the door of a dilapidated-looking wooden hut. Eve was among them, and Katie would have backed away, but Ross's hand was still at her waist, and she did not want to make a scene.

'Did you both get what you wanted?' the sneer on the redhead's face told Katie that she knew her ploy had worked, and she flushed, biting her lip to stem the sharp retort that rose on the tip of her tongue, but unwilling to give the other girl the satisfaction of seeing how upset she was.

'Yes, thank you,' she replied evenly, in as an indifferent a tone as she could muster, and had the satisfaction of seeing the other girl's blank look of surprise before she lowered her own eyes, to all intents and purposes absorbed in playing with the puppy in her arms, holding the ball Ross had given her above its tiny, snapping jaws in a game to while away the time they were forced to remain in the queue.

'You've bought the thing, you hold it.' Ross dumped the stuffed owl in her arms determinedly.

'I can't, I've got Quiz,' Katie cried, her voice muffled by a stiff mat of feathers under her chin. 'Let go!' as the puppy made a dive towards the unexpected arrival, and put itself and the owl in danger of being dropped.

'Then put the dog on his feet, you've got him on a lead,' Ross retorted. 'I'm going to fetch the goat,' he told her firmly, then seeing her difficulty he put his hand under the terrier's middle and supported him until he reached floor level. 'Now you can tuck that—thing—under your other arm,' he told her, 'and come along with me.' He opened the door of the pen that housed the goat and slipped inside, with a wary eye on the occupant which told her he was under no illusions as to its reaction to the rope collar he held in his hand. A quick slip of the wrist and the large black billy was firmly haltered, and to Ross's evident surprise it stepped meekly behind him out of the pen, to where he had drawn the Land Rover close alongside. A wooden gangplank made easy access to the back of the vehicle for their new purchase, which the moment it saw where it was expected to go reacted by living up to its bad name, and it was five hectic minutes before they managed to slam the door shut on its fiercely lowered head, and Ross and a sale yard helper wiped their foreheads and gazed with awe at the Land Rover, from which crashing sounds emerged with energetic regularity.

'Thank goodness there's a good stout grille between the front seats and the rest of the vehicle,' Katie voiced her thoughts feelingly. 'I hope it holds,' as another crash, louder than the others, made the sides of the Land Rover rattle.

'You're in for a hot journey home, guv'nor,' laughed the sale yard man. 'I don't envy you when you get to the other end, either,' he added.

'It should keep you pretty well occupied.' Eve's cool voice spun them round, and she smiled, her green eyes raking Katie and the stuffed owl prominent in her arms, so that she longed to forget herself, and hurl the efforts of the taxidermist at the auburn head. 'It will prevent you from—dallying—on the way,' she said sweetly, and spun on her heel towards her own vehicle parked nearby before Katie could think of a suitable retort.

CHAPTER FIVE

Unloading the goat was by no means as difficult as loading it up had been. Ross drew straight into the yard, where Ben had put up a roomy stockade, and the rest seemed incredibly easy after the stormy journey home.

'For goodness' sake, Quiz, be quiet!' Katie scolded the little dog as they drew out of the sale yard with their protesting load still rocketing about the back of the Land Rover in the most disconcerting manner. Katie glanced over her shoulder apprehensively, the steel grille between themselves and the goat looked suddenly over slender, and the puppy's near hysterical yapping at the large black creature it could see close by simply added to the din.

'Let him yap,' Ross advised, 'he's just what I want until we've brainwashed billy back there.' His eyes twinkled as he turned on to the lane that led back towards Mallets. 'It'll make him think he's a wonderful guard dog,' he encouraged. 'Go on, Quiz, speak!' His command had the effect of redoubling her pet's efforts and in the close confines of the cab, with the yapping puppy on her lap, there was no escape from the noise, which by the time they drew into the track that gave entrance to the farm had started a headache that Katie knew she would have cause to rule before long. 'Let him have another go before we leave the goat to it.' Ross took the pup's lead from her hand and led him towards the stockade, round which the goat was pacing stiff-legged as if it was looking for an exit, thought Katie, searching the stakes fearfully in case the creature found one. It was a long way to the gate in the garden wall, and she did not trust her legs to get there before the billy. 'Bark at him,' the man commanded, and nothing loth the pup gave tongue at the top of its voice, the noise spinning the goat round with an angry baaa which made Katie back a safe distance away.

'Don't be cruel!' she cried indignantly, wishing she had not let go of the pup's lead. 'Fancy penning a creature and then deliberately teasing it like that! It's—it's ...' She lost her voice, fury and disgust rendering her speechless. She had not thought Ross could be cruel, but here he was deliberately tormenting a helpless animal. 'Stop it!' she shouted, finding her voice, and at her frantic cry the man turned round. Slowly, he raised himself from his stooping position, slowly he gathered the puppy, silent now, into his arms, and from his superior height he looked down at Katie, seeing her swimming eyes across which she brushed a hasty hand, watching her flushed face and her trembling mouth for what seemed an age before he spoke.

'I'm not being cruel for fun, Katie.' His voice was soft, gentle, and he put his free hand about her shoulders, holding her to him and turning her away from the pen and out of the yard towards the little wicket gate in the garden wall, over which they had leaned and talked on her first night here. 'It's necessary for the safety of the sheep that that billygoat learns to hate dogs. That's why I let Quiz go on yapping at him. That's why I'm going to get Glen to bark at him each time he passes the stockade,' he told her, 'and after a few days of that treatment, when we put him in the field with the sheep he'll butt every dog in sight,' he said with satisfaction. 'In between times,' he told her with a small smile, 'I'm going to fuss him and feed him by hand, to try and make sure he doesn't do the same thing with human beings.'

'Do you mean that?' She asked it in a small voice choky with the violent upsurge of her feelings a moment ago, feelings that refused to believe Ross could be cruel, wanting to hate him and refusing to let her. Not knowing, in fact, what she wanted, only becoming aware as his touch calmed her in one way, that in another, deeper sense, she found it even more disturbing still, and about that she found she did not want to think.

'Whatever'ave you got there, Miss Katie?' Amy saved her from thinking for the moment, anyhow.

'It's an owl—a stuffed one.' Katie held it up for inspection, a small smile wavering on lips that rapidly became firmer as the smile gained a hold. 'I've got it for someone.' Despite her churning emotions she still did not intend to let Ross know for whom.

'I can't abide feathers,' Amy hastily defended herself against the possibility of being the recipient, and Katie's smile turned into a chuckle, which brought the man's eyes down to her face for an even longer moment than before.

'I'll put it on the shelf now,' she said mysteriously, 'and I'll put you in your basket,' she took hold of Quiz firmly. 'You've had quite enough new experiences for one morning.' And so have I, she added to herself feelingly, as she collapsed on her bed, and feeling the headache that had turned into what felt like violent hammer blows inside her skull quieten until it was no more than a dull pain behind her eyes, which she closed hoping it would go away, and opened with a start to find Amy beside her with a cup of tea and an anxious look on her face.

'I thought I'd come and see if you were all right, miss.' She indicated the clock, which

102

told Katie she had been sound asleep for at least a couple of hours.

'Goodness, the lunch!' Katie sat up and pushed her hair out of her eyes distractedly. 'I didn't intend going to sleep.'

'They've had their meal, miss, the men I mean,' Amy said comfortably. 'I gave them cold meat and mashed, the same as they usually has,' she said, and Katie settled back with her tea, conscious that her head had returned to normal, and that she was hungry. A small yawn from the basket beside her, and a shaking sound told her that Quiz was probably in the same state, and she swung herself on to her feet, her energy restored.

'I'll cut myself a quick sandwich, and then have a walk outside before I start getting the dinner ready,' she decided. 'Come on, Quiz.' She followed Amy downstairs, and took her own and the dog's meal on to the lawn outside the french windows. The strengthening sun made sitting out of doors pleasant, and she enjoyed her impromptu lunch, probably more than Ross had enjoyed his at Amy's hands, she thought with an inward twinkle. It would make him appreciate her own cooking all the more.

'Can I come and play wiv Quiz?' Two fair pigtails appeared over the garden wall minus their brown wooly cap, and their owner followed, clad in jeans and a tee-shirt, and carrying a black riding hat.

103

'For a few minutes, if you like,' Katie gave permission. 'Aren't you going riding?' she gestured towards the cap.

'In a minute, there's someone else having a lesson first.' Emma plonked herself on the grass at Katie's feet, her freckled face raised in a friendly fashion.

'I wanted to see you anyway,' Katie confided mysteriously, and was rewarded by an instant look of interest. 'When you go to Brownie meetings, do you still sit an owl on your toadstool and dance round it?' she raked up vague recollections from her own brief membership.

'Yes, but our owl's got no fevvers on,' Emma replied seriously, her diction hampered by the fact that three of her front teeth were missing. 'Brown owl said she'd get anuver, but ...' A small, eloquent shrug told Katie that the promise had not yet been fulfilled, and she breathed a sigh of relief.

'I know where there's one you can have.' She got to her feet, instantly followed by the child and the puppy. 'He's all yours.' She reached the stuffed bird down from its shelf and deposited it into the grasp of two thin, grateful arms. 'You can sit him on the grass while you have your riding lesson,' she suggested. That would be quite enough to tell Eve she had a purpose in bidding for the owl, she thought waspishly. If the purpose had made itself known after the bid, the auburn-haired riding mistress was not to know that, and small Emma's vociferous gratitude would leave the other woman in no doubt of it's destination, or its welcome there, she thought. 'I'll sit and mind him for you, and watch you ride,' she added, seeing the look of doubt on the small face, which cleared into a smile.

'The ponies eat things if you don't watch.' She cast a loving look at the owl, and Katie stifled a smile. It was hard to believe that the stuffed bird would have much attraction for a pony, she thought. Quiz, now, was a different matter; she had already lost a perfectly good slipper to his destructive teeth.

'Put him down here.' Katie folded her legs under her and sat on the grass just inside the five-barred gate, and watched with interest as Eve dealt with a circle of pupils riding the perimeter of a roped-off area nearby. 'Quiz can play by me, he won't come to any harm here,' she told her small companion. 'Put on your hat before you go,' she warned. 'If you take a tumble it'll save your head.'

'Miss Clements won't let us ride if we don't wear hard hats,' Emma said seriously, and smiled at Eve as she walked towards her next group of pupils patiently waiting by the gate.

'Of course not.' Eve gestured to the small girl to join the others. 'I know my job better than that,' she said in an aside to Katie, in a tone that added 'you needn't try to tell me

105

how to do it', and turning her back she supervised the children who were dismounting, checking each one as they came up and handed over the pony to the next in line.

'Not that way, boy. Mount up again, and dismount properly!' Her carrying voice floated back to Katie, who sat flushed and fuming, and but for the crowd at the gateway would have got up and gone back to the house. But she had promised Emma she would look after her owl, and also that she would watch her ride, and she did not want to disappoint the child, particularly when she had provided her with a ready-made home for her feathered mistake of the morning. She had seen Eve glance at it in a puzzled fashion, which made up a little for her own humiliation at the sale. It was a spiteful trick Eve had played on her, and she still smarted at her own gullibility. She waved as Emma mounted. Eve had to help her up, she noticed, her short legs could not cope, even with the diminutive pony she sat astride, but once up she seemed capable enough and sat her mount with easy confidence of a veteran.

'Wait for me, won't you?' she called back over her shoulder as she passed, leading the huddle of other ponies towards the roped-off circle. 'And you, Quiz,' she instructed the little dog.

At the sound of his playmate's voice the

puppy looked up, and saw that she was leaving him behind. With a quick yelp he took off, his short legs making surprising speed across the rough paddock grass, and Katie scrambled to her feet.

'Quiz, come back!' her urgent call went unheeded, and she started to run, but the small terrier was already in among the hooves of the ponies, causing a minor confusion among the animals as they tried not to step on him, and a major panic among their riders, who were evidently not as confident as Emma of keeping their seats on their now decidedly skittish mounts. One small boy began to cry, and his wail was taken up by another child on the edge of the group who Katie learned later was his sister, and as spoiled as he.

'Come here!' Eve reached the ponies before Katie, thrust her way into them with complete unconcern and grabbed Quiz by the scruff of his neck just as he reached Emma and tried to scrabble up a long chestnut leg to reach her outstretched hands.

'Don't hit him, Miss Clements. He's only trying to be friendly.' It was Emma's turn to wail now, but it had no effect on Eve, who delivered a sharp cuff before thrusting the puppy into Katie's outstretched arms, and looked as if she would dearly have loved to deliver another to its owner.

'For heaven's sake, have you got no sense?' she snapped. 'This thing,' she indicated a

107

very subdued Quiz, now cuddled in Katie's arms, 'could have caused a serious accident. If you can't keep it under control, stay out of the field,' she cried, her face white with a temper that did full justice to the colour of her hair.

'She came to watch me ride ...' Emma's voice verged on the tearful, and Eve made a gesture of impatience.

'You've come to be taught to ride, not to give a circus performance,' she said crushingly. 'Now for goodness' sake lead the others round the ring and let's not waste any more time.' She turned her back on Katie with deliberate rudeness, and walked after the last of the ponies, docile enough now, as they spread out quietly around the roped-off enclosure.

'She can't order me out of my own brother's field!' Katie turned furious eyes on Ross, who was approaching with a set look to his face that told her he had both seen and heard what went on.

'She can while she's renting it,' he said quietly, coming up beside her. 'And she's quite right, too. A puppy cavorting around under the ponies could easily cause one to bolt, Remember they're inexperienced children on top, not expert riders,' he told her shortly. 'Where's his halter?' he nodded at the pup. 'He'd be all right if he had that on, you could keep some sort of control then until he learns to come when you call him,' he said bluntly.

'It fidgeted him, so I took it off. I thought it would be all right for him to run free in the fields.'

'Not in this field,' Ross's voice was uncompromisingly stern. 'If you want to let him run free take him on to the lawns in the garden, or in any of the fields where there's no stock, until he's learned to behave. Anywhere else, keep him on the lead. And be sure to shut the gates behind you, or he'll be off.' To Katie's annoyance he checked that she had shut the wicket gate in the garden wall. 'He's small enough to go through a mousehole, nearly,' he added, and if there was a slight softening in his voice Katie was too angry to notice it. 'It's time you went in anyway, if we're going to have dinner by seven o'clock,' he threw at her, and turning on his heel strode towards Ben, who gestured to him from the yard that he needed help to move one of the chicken coops.

'Of all the ...' Katie went white, and found she was trembling, whether it was from fright in case the ponies might bolt—she had been very frightened, for a moment or two, for the same reason as Eve and Ross—or from anger, she did not try to analyse. She hated them both, she thought furiously. Anyone would think she had let the puppy run among the ponies on purpose, the possibility had never occurred to her, or she would have taken steps to make sure it did not happen—common sense should have told both Eve and Ross that. And knowing that, Eve need not have been so unpleasant. Or Ross, either, she thought, but he was bound to side with Eve. She hammered the steak for the dinner with quite unnecessary violence, making the cooking utensils rattle on the kitchen table, and Amy looked up from the sink.

'I've done the onions for you, if you're ready, miss?'

Katie held out her hands for the naked bulbs, glad of their strong aroma that gave her a legitimate excuse to wipe her eyes, aware that her helper looked at her sharply.

'At this rate we'll be well on time tonight,' she told Katie encouragingly. 'What about the sweet?'

'Oh, rhubarb and custard will do,' Katie replied indifferently. She did not really care whether they dined off fish and chips. She had no interest in either the cooking or the eating of the meal, her throat felt choked, and her tummy tied into a tight knot—that was what came of being angry, she told herself, and wondered even as she said it whether that was really the whole cause.

'There's a letter for you, by the late post,' Ross pointed out quietly as they sat opposite one another, Katie picking at her food in an uninterested manner, aware of nothing but the silence between them that was rapidly becoming unbearable. She started when Ross broke it, and looked up to find his eyes on her, watching her with a look of serious concern, but no anger. She had been half afraid he would still be angry, and now that her own temper had had time to evaporate she acknowledged that on the surface, he might have thought he had cause, an admission that gave her no comfort, and only added to the weight of depression that had settled on her and spoiled the sunny afternoon, and her pleasure in having the pup for company. She should have thought before she let Quiz loose, but his little legs seemed too tiny to run so fast, she would not have believed he could escape her grasp so easily. Ross had warned her that the breed was wilful, she would watch the little animal closely from now on, she vowed. But this determination did not wipe out the effects of the afternoon's unpleasantness, and the depression stayed with her still.

Her brother's letter did nothing to help. She slid it out from under her side plate where it had been placed in readiness for her arrival. That could not have been many minutes ago; she had seen the post van leave the farm just as she was dishing up the vegetables, and found it a small crumb of comfort that Ross was meticulous in this one

111

small, but important matter. She would have very much resented asking anyone, most of all him, for her mail.

'Go ahead and read it, you must be longing for his news.' He released her from consideration towards him, and she placed her knife under the flap and parted the envelope.

'He won't be able to start out for several more weeks yet.' She felt obliged to give her companion the news as well, since it affected him as much as it did herself.

'Is there anything wrong?' He gave her a tactful lead.

'No, here's what he says,' she read her brother's inky complaint. 'The infant doesn't seem in any hurry to join us. Wyn says not to worry, he'll come when he's ready and not before, but I'm afraid it will keep you tied longer than you may care. Let me know if it gets too inconvenient, though in the meantime you may find some paintable rural characters,' he encouraged hopefully. 'Pictures of Olde Englande, and that sort of thing . . .'

'That's an idea,' Ross took up the suggestion enthusiastically. 'You said that thatcher you met mending my roof had got an interesting face,' he reminded her.

'He'd got a paintable face,' corrected Katie musingly. Mark had unconsciously given her an incentive to settle down at Mallets until he

112

was able to come and take over, she realised gratefully. She had felt anything but settled until now, and this afternoon had had her casting about in her mind for an excuse to leave without causing bad blood between Ross and her brother when he eventually took over. 'I haven't brought any materials with me, but I can do some preliminary sketching.' It would while away the hours and give her an excuse to sit out in the sunshine as well, she thought, enlarging on the subject thankfully. It was one that she and Ross could discuss without referring back to the unfortunate events of the afternoon.

'I wouldn't mind having one of your paintings when it's finished,' he said unexpectedly. 'There must be a lot of things—people—you could use as subjects round here,' he hinted, and her mind flashed to Eve, the red hair piled high, her open necked shirt slightly too well fitting on her slender figure, and her green eyes a venomous contrast that somehow managed still to leave her face uninterestingly empty of character. No doubt he would like a painting of Eve, she thought disparagingly, but he would not get one by her brush. She'd rather paint Amy, at least her face was amiable, whereas when she was near Katie, Eve's face was not.

'I'll see what your thatcher says,' she hedged. 'He seems friendly enough, but he may not like being put on to canvas. Lots of

113

people don't,' she said vaguely, determined not to be drawn into a promise to do a portrait for him. She felt if she started a portrait of his girl-friend it might end up with a furry face that would purr when stroked ... Now I'm being catty, she told herself, but unrepentantly. The brush with the riding mistress rankled, as did Ross's attitude afterwards.

'Now eat your dinner,' he told her, rather as if she was one of the children at the riding school, she thought resentfully, but just the same Mark's letter had broken the silence between them, and she found her appetite had returned with the easier atmosphere, enabling her to tackle her food with enough energy to satisfy him. 'If you starve yourself,' he told her, 'you'll have Amy clucking round you like a mother hen.'

'Talking about hens,' she remembered Ben had called him, 'did you manage to move the chicken coop?' She was not really interested, but it was better than the silence coming back.

'Yes.' He took the rhubarb and custard from Amy, spooned some into a dish for Katie without asking her whether she wanted any or not, then helped himself. He evidently intended to see that she finished the rest of her meal, and she felt too listless to make any real effort to refuse; it was easier to swallow it without comment. Besides, it gave her something to do while she thought out Mark's suggestion, that despite herself took hold of her imagination.

'Yes, Ben wanted the chickens back in the bull's pen,' Ross said conversationally, as if he, too, was glad that the silence had been routed. 'He took them out to give them more room, although they're young cockerels, well past the stage of being chicks, and they can quite well manage to get in and out of the stable themselves now when they want to,' he told her. 'They come back to the pen at night, the same as the others.'

'You'd think the bull would object,' Katie said curiously, her interest aroused.

'It's for his sake we keep them in there,' Ross responded. 'Animals like company, and he's no exception. Fowl create a diversion,' his eyes smiled mischievously. 'They're a bit like women really,' he jibed softly, 'they're scattery creatures, and there's always an uproar of some sort when they're around. It keeps the other—animals—interested,' he put slight emphasis on the word 'animals', and Katie flushed, resenting the implication that she might be 'scattery'. Jeremy Bailey had pinned the same label on her before they'd even met, dubbing her 'artist' and not even bothering to think beyond the conventional image. In him it was perhaps excusable, as he had the responsibility of Mallets on his hands, and dared not take any risks, but Ross should have known her better by now, she thought furiously.

'You go a pretty pink when you're angry.' His eyes laughed at her across the table. 'It becomes you . . .' He lapsed into hasty silence as Amy's foot thudded on the bottom of the dining room door, preceding her appearance in the room with a tray of coffee things.

'I thought you'd like your coffee in here tonight.' She waited for Ross's nod before she put the tray down on the table. 'Ben said you wanted to go out and feed the goat last thing, so I've saved him some greenstuff,' she said practically, 'and a bit of stale cake in case he's partial to sweet stuff. You never know, it might make him more amiable,' her tone implied that she doubted the possibility, but was willing to do her bit in the attempt.

'I told you I was going to feed that billy by hand,' Ross included Katie in the conversation. 'He must have a soft spot somewhere, and piece of cake might just reach it.' He smiled at Amy gratefully and was rewarded by a beam in return. Really, Ross could be quite nice when he chose, thought Kate sourly; it was only when he and she were together they seemed to bring out the worst in each other. Maybe they were both prejudiced from the start, she acknowledged, and gathered together every ounce of her considerable self-discipline to put on an amiable front while Amy was in the

116

room.

'You're not going into the pen with him?' she looked at him aghast, and wondered if she rather wished he would. It would give her a lot of satisfaction. 'I thought you might care to come along and feed him as well.' The gleam deepened. 'The more people he gets used to the better. That is, if you're not nervous?'

It was a direct challenge, and Katie's chin came up. The thought of facing the billy, even from the safe side of the enclosure, made her quake, but she would not let Ross see that she was even the alightest bit worried by the prospect, and she grasped the piece of cake that Amy gave her in a hand that she hoped was not obviously trembling, and followed Ross out to the pen. As they approached it the billy spun round and faced them, his head lowered threateningly, and she paused, but Ross walked quietly on and she forced her reluctant legs to follow him. The goat watched them warily, but seemed to be looking for something else as well.

'He's looking for Glen,' Ross told her quietly. She noticed he had shut the dog in the kitchen when they came out, an unusual thing as the two were almost invariably to be seen together. 'It's all right, old chap, there isn't a dog in sight.' He spoke soothingly to the goat, reaching out a hand and holding his offering up for it to see. The animal paused

117

hesitated, and after when to Katie seemed an eternity came forward, its nose sniffing the handful of succulent greenstuff. It nibbled, with a wary eye on Ross, but when he remained immovable it began to eat with evident enjoyment. 'In a day or two, when he's got used to this, I'm going to try scratching his head,' he murmured. At the sound of his voice the busy jaws stopped, but as Ross continued talking it must have decided that there was no threat from the direction of the sound, because it finished the greenstuff without another pause. 'Now your cake.' There was a slight return of his grin, which gave Katie the necessary courage to lean over the rails and thrust her hand out towards the big black head. It reached forward, sniffing, and she succumbed to her instinct. She shut her eyes tightly. She felt snuffling breath on her fingers, and held her own with a little gasp which she could not quite control, but nothing hapened beyond a satisfied champing sound, and she opened one eye a fraction and took a wary peep.

'Your hand's still there,' an amused voice assured her from above her head, 'but if you don't let him have the last bit of cake your fingers might not be, soon!' Katie realised with astonishment that the large piece of cake was reduced to a small and rapidly diminishing crust in her fingers, and she transferred it to the tips with unseemly speed.

'Let me give him the last bit.' Ross was openly laughing at her now, and he prised apart her fingers and shook the last bit of cake into his own palm, adroitly transferring it to the goat's jaws with a coolness that Katie tried not to admire. 'You're a fighter, I'll say that for you.' A tinge of admiration replaced the amusement in his voice, and Katie looked up quickly. The gleam in his eyes had gone, at least the mocking, challenging gleam, and she looked away, not sure what the expression she read in them now meant.

'Are you going back to the house now?' She busied herself wiping the cake crumbs from her fingers, not wanting to look at him, not wanting him to look at her, because she found his look had become a disturbance which, once more, she did not want to acknowledge.

'Not until I've checked on the rest of the stock. I might as well do the rounds while I'm out.' Katie knew he or Ben always came out at about this time, near dusk, to finally shut up for the night, and she walked along with him, suddenly reluctant to go back to the house herself. She did not feel like her own company just now. Without any reason that she could analyse, she felt on edge, her emotions jumbled up in the most inexplicable manner. She supposed it was the upset with Eve during the afternoon, and the fright she had felt in case Quiz caused one of the ponies to bolt, her throat still constricted at the thought. Added to that the news in Mark's letter was disappointing; it was a let-down she had not anticipated, and the prospect of an even longer stay at Mallets in the rather negative position into which the solicitor's action of putting Ross in charge had driven her was not something that she particularly relished. Certainly now she had taken over the meals she had something to do, and Quiz would provide her with a pleasant occupation for the rest of the time, but she still felt superfluous to the running of the place, even if Ross did openly express his appreciation at the changeover from Amy's cooking to her own.

'I'll have to get some sketching paper.' She spoke her thoughts out loud, her mind running on Mark's suggestion of a series of sketches of rural characters. Silently she blessed her brother for the idea. It had not occurred to her, but now her stay here was prolonged she was glad of something to occupy her mind as well as her hands.

'Has it got to be anything special?' Ross tuned in easily to her wavelength, and spoke in a friendly, conversational tone, as if he too was interested in the idea. Probably interested in keeping her occupied, and thus out of his way, thought Katie glumly, but nevertheless it provided a neutral ground where they could converse without growling at one another, she realised thankfully. This eternal sparring that had dominated their relationship since the moment they met—on her part, before they met—was beginning to get on her nerves, and the extra weeks to which her new relative's late arrival had condemned her had begun to look more like a sentence than a time of waiting.

'Not necessarily, any reasonable paper would do, providing it's of a good size. Perhaps the village shop has got some children's drawing books. I've got my own pencils, I'm never without them in case I see something particularly interesting, but I hadn't bargained on having time on my hands when I got here.' She could not help the thrust and was vexed with herself the moment it was uttered. The last thing she wanted to do was to let Ross realise she was even the slightest bit put out by her displacement at his hands. That was unfair, she knew. It was at Jeremy Bailey's instigation he had come, but she was not in a mood to be fair, and she felt unrepentant. 'I can do the paintings afterwards from the preliminary sketches and notes,' she enlarged. 'There's a publisher I know who might be interested,' she went on, warming to the idea, preferring a reason for her work before she started on it, since it provided an added incentive beyond her own keen interested. 'He's asked me several times to illustrate books for him, and I've never been able to fit it in, and I know he's commissioned one of country life generally, so a series of paintings like this might just fit the bill for him.'

'That sounds a grand idea.' Ross's voice rose enthusiastically. Whether it was genuine enthusiasm or not Katie did not feel like probing; it was sufficient to keep their relationship on an even keel and give some common ground on which they could talk. 'But about the paper, there's a fair sized block of it in your grandfather's desk.' It rankled, him talking like this, thought Katie, trying to subdue the prickly feeling that always rose inside her when he spoke in such a familiar way about things that she considered it was her own place to be aware of, not his. 'It's about a foot square, probably a little larger,' he guessed, 'but I didn't know whether a professional like yourself might be fussy about the materials you use.'

'Very fussy, about the materials for the finished job,' Katie rejoined drily, 'but I have been known to do sketches on the backs of old envelopes in an emergency,' she added, glancing up at him with a look that suspected sarcasm, but there was none there, although the fading light shaded the expression in his eyes, so that she could not see if the now familiar challenging gleam was in them or not.

'Then the paper in your grandfather's desk should do admirably,' he retorted. 'I'm going to shut up the bull, you needn't come any further if you don't want to.' The challenge was back in his voice, and drew the expected response from Katie.

'I'll stay with you,' she determined, thinking it unnecessary to add that if she waited for him where she was it was a good deal too close for her liking to the pen that held the gander, which seemed even at this late time in the day inclined to hiss at her in an unwelcoming fashion. We're all at it, she thought miserably, biting at one another with an aggression that seemed quite unjustified in this peaceful spot.

'You needn't come into Buttercups stable,' he excused her with a smile. 'I'm only going into drop the hatch on the fowl pen.'

'Are you afraid of the bull stepping on them or something?'

'No, I just don't want them flying straight into Ben's face when he opens the top half of the stable door in the morning,' retorted Ross, scratching the bull's nose that it held up in a friendly fashion for what was evidently an accustomed fuss. 'Back up a bit, and let me through,' he told the creature, and as it moved away he slipped through the bottom half of the door, which Katie noticed he instantly bolted behind him before he leaned down to the hen coop in a corner of the stable, and dropped the hatch to the floor. The routine chore done, he gave the bull's nose another rub, whereupon it ambled back into its own side of the stable, allowing him to rejoin Katie on the walkway outside, and shut and bolt both parts of the door safely for the night.

'Can't Ben do the locking up for you at night?' Katie would have thought it to be his responsibility rather than Ross's.

'He does usually, but he's in the darts team at the local, and there's a big match on tonight,' Ross said easily, 'so I've stepped in for him.' He bent and tested the firmness of the pen that enclosed the gander, and Katie noticed with satisfaction that the occupant hissed at him with the same fervour that it had used towards herself. 'That's on some fairly loose soil,' he hesitated, scraping the ground into a small mound with the toe of his shoe.

'Surely he's not one of the great escapers?' Katie felt suddenly tired, and curiously depressed, and contrarily wanted to go inside to the warmth of the fire that each night Amy considerately lit in the drawing room, conscious of the chill that can invade stone houses after even the warmest of days. She shivered, feeling it now, even outside.

'No, but . . .' Ross still hesitated, his hand on the top spar of the pen.

'You promised to show me where that paper was, in Grandfather's desk,' Katie reminded him, and he straightened, loosening his hold on the pen.

'I'll get Ben to see to that in the morning,' he murmured, noticing her shiver again. 'You're cold—it's time we went in.' He took her by the elbow and steered her towards where the wicket gate gleamed whitely in the garden wall, so that whatever was wrong with the pen could not have been all that important, Katie judged, or he would not have left it simply because he had seen her shiver. She could not think he would bother whether she was cold or not if he had anything else of the least importance to attend to, and she did not imagine that she could possibly be as important to Ross as the gander, she thought caustically, her mood made less intractable by the fact that his touch upon her arm brought with it a curious warmth, that illogically made her shiver again, but this time it had nothing to do with the temperature of the approaching night.

CHAPTER SIX

The block of paper in her grandfather's desk had been just right. Katie left it on the top where she could reach it easily, and remembered Ross's promise of the night before.

'If you're going sketching out of doors,

you'll want something to bear on. And a clip of some sort to keep the sheets from blowing about. I'll see if I've got a piece of board that will do,' he promised.

He was getting it for her now. He had passed her on the landing, commented smilingly upon her early rising habits, and said he would make it his first job to find her the promised board. Ben could do the round of the yard himself that morning.

'Gaffer! Where's gaffer got to?' Hasty footsteps clattered on the quarry floor of the kitchen, and Ben's voice could be heard demanding information from the placid Amy.

'I dunno. Ask Miss Katie, he's gone to get her something.'

'He's gone to find me a piece of board.' Katie thrust the kitchen door open and poked her head inside. 'Why, Ben, what's the matter?' The farmhand looked flustered and upset. 'Can I do anything?' she asked hopefully.

'I dunno as anyone can do anything, Miss Katie,' Ben replied feelingly, 'but you'd best come and see.' He turned and hastened out again, and Katie followed him, with a quick, inquiring look at Amy that was met by a shrug and upraised hands as if to say that whatever had happened, it was none of her doing. 'Look at that now, will you?' He pointed an eloquent finger at the pen that held the gander. 'It's that blamed fox as 'as

126

done that, I'll be bound, and me thinking it wouldn't hurt for the one night,' he reproached himself. 'It wouldn't have taken a minute or two, but I was that keen to get off to me darts match...'

'How did you get on?' Katie tried to distract him. The gander that had hissed at her the night before was now horribly, obviously dead, its long neck outstretched to where a hole had been scraped under the side of the pen in the soft, loose soil that Ross had scraped with the toe of his shoe the night before. There were other scratch marks there now, long, narrow ones, and a heap of soil where the digger had scattered it behind out of its way so that it could wriggle through the hole and get to its victim.

'We won.' The minor triumph had turned to ashes in Ben's mouth, and his victory brought him no comfort. 'I'd just as soon we lost, rather than 'ave this 'appen.' Misery made him forget his aitches in a way that, had Amy been near, would have brought a dig of reproof from her elbow.

'It's not your fault,' Katie protested. 'Who'd dream of a fox scratching under a pen like this?' She regarded the scene with a small shudder. 'And it wasn't able to drag the gander out after all.' The waste as well as the horror struck her.

'He wouldn't be able to. The wing's 'as spread out against the bars, see? The harder he pulled 'un by the neck the harder the wings stuck against the wood. I blames meself . . .' Ben looked at her, self-reproach clouding his usually bright, alert morning face.

'Then you shouldn't. It's my fault.' Ross's voice brought them both round to face him, where he stood just behind them, viewing the scene with a grim look. 'I penned up last night,' he reminded Ben, 'and I saw the soil was loose under this one. I scraped it with my toe, and then decided to leave it until the morning I went indoors instead, to—er—do something else.' The fact that Katie was present dawned on him, and she flushed.

'You went because I asked you to,' she reminded him, 'to get the paper from Grandfather's desk for me.' So really it was her fault that this thing had happened. She gulped, her face taking on a reflection of Ben's expression, and Ross scowled at them both.

'Don't be reidiculous, either of you,' he snapped at them both. 'Foxes have been taking fowl from the time the world began, and unless we catch this one he'll have more, now he's discovered how easy it is to tunnel in to them,' he prophesied. 'The only thing we can do is to catch the fox. And give the gander to the ladies to cook,' he added briskly.

'I'll pluck and dress 'un for you.' Ben hastened to make amends for his guilt, and

128

Katie smiled at him gratefully averting her eyes from the pathetic dead thing at their feet. It was easy enough obtaining fowl from the butcher, they were naked, anonymous and seemed to have no real relation to a living, clucking hen, but this was something different. Last night the gander had been full of vital, aggressive life, Katie remembered the look in its eye as it hissed at her, not unlike the gleam in Ross's eye as he challeneged her to feed the billygoat, she thought, and did her best to summon up an indifferent air of a cook who merely sees the making of a good dinner.

'Do that,' she told Ben with as much cheerfulness as she could muster, 'and I'll make you something special for tonight. Something plain,' she hastened to add, as unenthusiasm joined gloom on his face, and he brightened up visibly.

'Have you got any idea where the fox might be holed up?' Ross gazed at the surrounding countryside reflectively. 'It's probably a vixen with cubs,' he added.

'I reckon up in them rocks.' Ben gestured towards where the sharp outcrop of rock reared against the smiling sky, mocking its blue summer beauty with harsh, uncompromising lines. 'There was a vixen holed up there in a little cave when I wur a lad,' he remembered, 'an' this one, she's been nuisance for long enough and no one's managed to flush her out yet, so she could be in the same lair.'

'We'll try, immediately after breakfast. I'll take Glen,' promised Ross.

'He'll be too big to get inside the crack in the rock,' warned Ben. 'I'll go and fetch our Alf's little terrier. He's a Jack Russell, like yours, Miss Katie,' he explained, suddenly able to talk to her without confusion, drawn out of his shell by the emergency.

'What can he do?' Katie was curious, fondling Quiz's tiny body and wondering how something so small would fare against a fox.

'Flush the animal out of its lair,' Ross responded. 'If it's holed up in that little cave behind a crack in the rocks up there, as Ben says,' he gestured with his breakfast fork to where the rock reared upwards in the distance beyond the dining room window, 'then we shall have to drive it out before we can deal with it.' He did not say how he intended to deal with it, and Katie forbore to ask, but she was curious about the men using the terrier, just the same.

'They seem so small,' she protested. 'You said Quiz would only grow to about fourteen inches.'

'Yes, but he'll be fourteen inches of fighter, don't forget. A bit like his present owner,' Ross grinned, and was rewarded by a flash in Katie's eyes that warned of retaliation if he should give her half a chance. 'They're

130

working dogs, Katie,' his tone altered and became serious, 'and it's just those properties of courage and fighting spirit that make men use them for such jobs as these.'

'Jobs they can't do themselves.' Katie's jibe was soft but deadly.

'Because we can't wriggle through narrow gaps in between rocks,' Ross pointed out, in no way put out, to her annoyance. 'Come along with us, and you'll see what I mean. You can always close your eyes if you don't like what's happening.' His grin was back, reminding her unkindly of when she fed the goat.

'I won't bring Quiz,' she decided, dropping him into his basket with a quick instruction to Amy to watch him while she was away.

'I'll put a few extra cartridges in my pocket, just in case.' Ross rummaged in the writing desk while Katie slipped on her windcheater. He did not say in case of what, and she refused to be drawn, watching in silence as he unhooked a gun from the rack fixed to the wall above the desk. Her eyes caught sight of a square of polished wood resting on the pile of papers she had put on the top for when she wanted to sketch. It had two large elastic bands crossed over the back, so that they clipped the corners on the front of the board in a manner that would hold any paper she put on the board firmly and without creasing, and without interfering

131

with her sketching space.

'What a good idea!' She fingered the simple but effective paper holder with appreciative fingers. 'And a nice piece of board, too.' It was smooth and flat, with no rough patches on its surface, and nothing to catch on the sides, which had been smoothed to the texture of glass. A powdering of sawdust along one edge told Katie that Ross had had to saw it to size, but that edge, too, had been carefully rubbed down so that there were no splinters to damage her fingers, and she turned a delighted face in his direction.

'That will do beautifully,' she thanked him, and he bowed mockingly, but not before she had caught the pleased look on his face that told her he was glad she liked the results of his efforts.

'My pleasure,' he murmured. 'Coming, Ben.' He thrust a handful of cartridges into his pocket and paused. 'It's a long, uphill walk,' he warned her.

'I'm tough,' she assured him, and he nodded, accepting the fact that she intended to come as well.

'Come on, then, the sooner we get it over the better.' The tone of his voice held distaste, and Katie hesitated, but she was determined not to back out now, and firmly thrusting away her qualms she stepped out after him. Ben was waiting for them, just outside the kitchen door, and he, too, carried a gun slung easily in the crook of his arm, and Katie stared at him in surprise. Suddenly the mild, inarticulate farmhand had changed, and she was not too sure that she liked the change—in either of her companions. She looked from one to the other, seeing determined men sallying forth to protect their livestock in just such a manner as their ancestors must have had to protect their beasts, indeed their very homes and families, from the threat of molestation and even death, and although modern thinking gave each of them a distaste for the task ahead of them, she knew it would not prevail against the primitive hunter's instinct and the need to protect what was their own.

They walked at a reasonable pace, but more, she felt, to ensure the small dog that trotted beside them did not tire unduly before they got to the rocks than with any chivalrous instinct towards herself, which in any case she did not need, as she found she could keep up with them easily. The soft, rolling rises of the wold country made gentle hills, it was only as the upthrust of harder rock rose closely before them that she realised they had some really steep climbing to do if they were to reach an outcrop to which Ben pointed as holding the cave he remembered from long ago.

'It's years since I was up here,' he confessed, 'but I've wondered for long enough if it might be where that vixen has holed up. She's got away too often from her raids, and there's been no trace of her afterwards.'

'She's probably travelled upstream, along the Burley Brook,' Ross agreed. 'It starts up here somewhere as a spring, so it would make an ideal cover to eliminate any scent.'

Katie felt she would like to paddle in it now. The warmth of the sun flung heat back at them from the rock underfoot, something they had not noticed on the soft grass, and she slipped off her windcheater, glad of the cool of the breeze on her arms. The small terrier ran on ahead, nose to the ground, casting about them in rough scrub and gorse that somehow found a living on the inhospitable slope and would provide excellent cover, Katie realised, for any number of foxes, not just one.

'Here!' Ben called it to heel sharply, and it checked immediately, coming back to him with a quiet obedience that was stronger than its urge to investigate scents of paramount interest to a doggy nose. Ross looked back at Katie, and smiled slightly, as if to say, 'That's how you should train Quiz,' but he did not speak, only his smile broadened as Katie made a face at him, reading his message but too out of breath to retaliate verbally. Just the same such evidence of patient training on someone's part—doubtless the 'our Alf' of

Ben's conversation earlier—impressed her strongly, and for Quiz's sake as well as that of her family she determined to be firm with the little dog entrusted to her care until they arrived. Ross had warned her, and she had already had one example—it could have been a disastrous one—of the consequences if he was allowed to ignore her call.

'Phew!' She paused for a moment to get her breath, and Ross stopped too, waiting for her to catch him up.

'You're tired,' he accused her. 'I told you it would be a long pull up here.'

'I'm not tired!' Katie found enough breath to sound indignant. 'I'm just hot, that's all,' she stated valiantly. 'And it seems a long way to come when you don't even know if there'll be a fox when you get there.'

'We had to come to find out,' he pointed out reasonably enough. 'We can't just do nothing and let the animal go on killing the stock. Your brother will expect to find something occupying the fowl pens when he arrives to take over,' he added, with a note of impatience in his voice that gave her sadistic pleasure, since it told her he was feeling as hot as she was, and just as reluctant to let it show.

'The vixen's here right enough!' Ben point ahead to a bare patch of ground immediately in front of the final high crag of rock that arose huge and sheer from a clutter of

135

boulders about its base, proclaiming she could not guess how many years of storm that at this height would carry a violence strong enough to bring down loose rocks such as these. Even now, the wind blew cold, stirring the tangle of browny red feathers to which Ben pointed, lifting it casually so that it spread in the semblance of the fowl's wing it once was, then dropping it back again on the rocks as if contemptuous of its lack of life.

'We lost a couple of Rhode Island Reds over a week ago,' Ben's voice was grim, and he shaded his eyes against the sun to scan the rock for the gap he was seeking. 'There it is,' he pointed ahead of them to where a slender dark slit showed up clearly as they approached.

'You wouldn't think a fox could get through that.' Katie eyed it in surprise.

'They don't need a lot of room,' Ross replied, 'they're as agile as cats, and they can squeeze through holes a lot smaller than that, if necessary. That's where the terrier comes in.' He snapped his fingers, and the grown-up replica of Quiz came trotting towards him eagerly, with a soft whine that told him it knew its quarry was close by. Ross pointed the little dog in the direction of the slit in the rock, and waited. He did not need to wait for long. With a quick, eager sound in its throat that made Katie shiver and slide her arms back into her anorak, it bounded towards the slit, and with a scrabbling of paws on rock it disappeared into the darkness inside. Ross followed up behind, and Katie stepped alongside him, suddenly not wanting to be on her own. Her foot slipped on something round, that rolled away, and she saw with a shudder that it was a sheep's skull, its eyeholes gaping circles of blankness.

'The fox wouldn't have killed that,' Ross spoke quietly seeing her expression. 'I expect it fell, the sheep clamber up here and then can't get down.' He stopped abruptly as a series of snarls emerged from the hole in the rock, and quietly slipped a cartridge into his gun, which he shut with a final-sounding click. 'Let's go and stand with Ben.' Ross took her arm and drew her to where the farmhand stood a little distance away. 'The dog will flush the vixen out with a bit of luck, and it isn't safe to shoot standing opposite to one another.' He came to a halt and swung round facing the rock as the sounds of fierce battle came from inside the entrance. Growls punctuated with snarls and now and then a high-pitched yap from the terrier screwed Katie's nerves to cracking point, and she put her hands to her ears, unable to stand it any longer, on the instant that a long, sleek body catapulted out of the entrance to the cave, followed without pause by the stumpy form of the terrier. As soon as it hit the ground outside the fox spun to face the dog, and Ross raised his gun, then immediately lowered it again as the terrier flung itself at the fox, seeking a hold on its adversary's throat.

The wild creature staggered back under the onslaught, caught temporarily off balance, and its one paw caught on the sheep's skull, jamming itself in the gap of one of the eye sockets, that was large enough to let it through, but tight enough to hold it when it was there. Frantically the fox shook its paw, attempting to throw off the encumbrance, and the moment of inattention was just what the terrier was looking for. From the advantage of its smaller size it leapt upwards, its teeth gripping the vixen's throat and the temporarily exposed area of the vital jugular vein. The two animals rolled over, oblivious of the watching humans. Hampered by the restriction on its leg, and unable to shake off the death grip on its throat, the fox rapidly lost strength, its breath coming in great, wheezing gasps that flecked itself and its attacker with blood. The end came quickly. With a final paroxysm of fury that gave added strength to its jaws, and the terrier triumphed. A shudder shook the wild, red body, and the vixen collapsed, hate blazing from the amber eyes one moment, the next a blankness without feeling.

'There's cubs still in there, gaffer.'

Katie suddenly felt sick. Her knees trembled, and she sat down hurriedly on a nearby rock, turning her back to the terrier, which the moment it had despatched its victim shook itself matter-of-factly and trotted up to the farmhand, in a manner that clearly asked whether it should finish the job it had set out to do.

'Go on, then.' Ben sent it about its business, as matter-of-fact as the dog, and Katie dropped her face into her hands, trying with her fingers to stifle the sounds of baby distress that came from behind her, but quickly ceased.

'Is that the lot?'

Ross's voice sounded far away, and she unstuffed her ears, bringing the world back to her, the normal sane everyday world where the sound of the wind made a background to the scuffing of men's feet on the rock and the hard scrabble of the terrier's paws. From somewhere below them a lamb called, its voice high-pitched and seeking, as if it had lost sight of the ewe. It called twice more, then was silent as if the familiar, comforting presence was beside it again, and Katie lifted her face from her hands, and felt them wet.

'I shouldn't have brought you.' Ross's voice was contrite, his hands gentle as he raised her from the rock and she leaned against him for a moment, unsure of her balance until the crisp coolness of the wind stung returning colour to her cheeks and she stood with more confidence on her own. Still

139

Ross kept his one arm about her, and she turned within it.

'Don't look...'

But she had to. Some compulsion made her turn round and see for herself what had happened, before they came away; face the awful reality of it rather than the even more awful wondering of how it had ended, that she felt would haunt her dreams if she did not know. There were four cubs.

'That's the lot, gaffer.' Ben spoke, and his voice was quiet, too. 'I can see right to the back of the den she had, and there's nothing else in it.'

With a compassion she would not have suspected of him, considering his earlier determination to accomplish the results she now looked upon, Ben placed the small bodies beside that of the vixen, and turned with them downhill.

'Alf and me'll come up afterwards, and bury 'un,' he jerked his thumb back over his shoulder, then stooped and gathered the terrier into his arms, examining it thoroughly. 'Only one bite, I'll bathe it as soon as we get home.' He put it down to the ground again and let it run free, and it turned downhill with never a backward glance to where the fitful wind fingered the fowl's wing, stirring it along the rock so that it came to rest almost within reach of the cubs who had used it as a plaything, contending with one another for possession of it until they tired of their game and sought something else to interest them in their barren lair. Finding no response, the wind tossed it closer, ruffling the baby fur that made a golden halo about the tiny bodies, not unlike the gold tips around Katie's own head; with a quick spin the dusty feathers brushed against the nearest cub, enticing it to action, the breeze pushing the discarded toy teasingly against paws that no longer wanted to play.

'Shall I see to the gander for you, Miss Katie? I can get it done in time if you want it for dinner tonight,' Ben offered as they neared the yard gate.

'No!' Katie felt she would really be sick if she had to cope with the gander today. Or at any other time. Vivid pictures of it and the fate of its killer spun through her mind in dizzy confusion, and she began to tremble.

'Give it to Alf, will you, Ben?' Ross spoke quietly, his hand on her shoulder. 'It'll be a sort of thank you for borrowing his dog,' he pointed out, and Ben beamed.

'He'll be right pleased, gaffer. Thanks very much.' Evidently Ben regarded the offer as almost a gift to himself, and he departed whistling.

'Now come inside and have a cup of tea.' Ross's hand tightened its grasp, and she looked up, drawing back from the house.

'I don't want anything to eat—I couldn't.'

'I'm not suggesting you eat,' although it was lunchtime, she realised with a quick glance at her watch. 'I don't want anything either, but a drink would be welcome, and you can take your sketching block down to the Lodge for the afternoon afterwards,' he suggested. 'It'll be a good idea to try the board and to see if it's suitable, and I've made you a running lead for Quiz, so that you can let him run free while you're sketching. It'll save you bothering one another,' he added with a slight smile, and she stirred.

'I'll make the tea.' She did not feel like it, but the simple task steadied her, and while she was about it she cut a plate of sandwiches. She did not want to eat, but she could not expect Ross to go hungry; he was always up at the crack of dawn and needed his food. Gradually her fingers ceased to tremble, so that she wielded the knife with more confidence, the very normality of the kitchen, and Amy's cheerful chatter bringing the events of the morning into perspective.

'Don't worry about Ben, I'm giving him a fry of bacon and eggs. He was that upset this morning, he only had half his breakfast,' Amy told her, sparing her the task of preparing lunch for the other two, and freeing her to collect her sketching materials and Quiz for the afternoon outing. She felt thankful for Ross's suggestion, it would provide just the antidote she needed for the horror of the morning. Another time, she vowed, she would leave such matters to the men to deal with, and checked herself hastily. She was thinking ahead as if she was going to stay at Mallets and of course she was not. She would be going away again soon—would be glad to go, she had told herself so time and time again—so there would be no more seasons here when she would be expected to cope with fox damage, no more springs when she would walk the wolds with Ross, or lean on the garden wall beside him and watch the dusk creep across the water fields that bordered the Burley Brook.

A lump rose in her throat, and she nodded, unable to speak when Amy asked her if she had got everything she needed on her laden tray.

'Eh, Miss Katie, the men shouldn't've taken you along with them this morning, you're fair upset.' Amy's concern came close to upsetting her still further, and she sighed with relief as Quiz appeared, bustling through the door in search of her.

'I should have had more sense than to go,' Katie admitted, finding her voice. 'Come along, out of Amy's way.' She toed the door open, a habit she found she was catching from her helper, and shooed the pup through it. 'We'll be out sketching this afternoon,' she told her, 'so you'll be able to enjoy a bit of peace.'

'And so will you, if you tie him to this.' Ross accepted his cup of tea with a murmur of thanks—he was invariably polite, even if he was annoyed with her, Katie noticed—and held up two stout wire stakes around which was bound a considerable quantitiy of cord. 'There's another piece here, to tie to his halter,' he held up a further roll with a large loop at one end. 'You can drive the stakes into the ground, let the noose run along the cord in between them, and he'll have an area to run in big enough to satisfy even his sense of curiosity,' he told her with a smile.

'What a good idea!' Katie examined his offering, pleased with the kindly thought behind it, even if that thought had only been for the puppy, and not for her. Suddenly, wistfully, she found herself wishing it might have been a little for her sake as well. Ross could be wonderfully gentle, she had discovered. Utterly ruthless, too, when necessary, as their morning's trip had shown, but he made no attempt to hide his dislike of what he had had to do then; he was strong enough to admit without shame to what others might regard as weakness, she thought, and the fact that he had in part shared her revulsion was probably the cause of his consideration to her as they walked back to the farm. She could feel the pressure of his hand on her shoulder still, calm, comforting, regretting the action they had

had to take, but not shrinking from the necessity of it, and hard on the heels of her previous wish came another, so unexpected that it caught her unawares, and left her wondering why she should wish that things could have been otherwise for herself and Ross.

That they might, perhaps, have met under different circumstances, where they could both have been free to get to know and like one another, unhampered by the antagonism that she herself had felt towards him even before they met, and he had probably sensed in her, and reacted by an impatience that made her feel an unwelcome nuisance in her grandfather's house; where he might have been free of any ties—the thought of Eve touched her with a cold finger. She could not blame him for wanting to marry the girl; to most men she would appear beautiful, with her slender carriage, and that Titian hair that she flaunted like a flag to attract Ross's glance, and warn herself, Katie, away. Perhaps it was only her artist's eye that sought something extra in Eve's face, or underneath its surface, some sign that might proclaim a warm human being behind the beautiful exterior, rather than the cold self-seeking that her woman's instinct suspected, and found repellent.

'You should be able to push these wire stakes into the ground easily enough,' Ross was saying, and she came back to her surroundings with a sense of unreality, so deep had been her thoughts. 'Or maybe not.' He regarded her small hands thoughtfully, 'The ground's a bit hard with the dry weather. I'll walk along with you as far as the Lodge,' he made up his mind suddenly. 'I've got to go there sometime today anyway, to check on some new stock my farm manager bought last week.' So he had a farm manager. Katie realised dimly that this heir to the Heseltine acres was a man of some substance, despite the fact that he had had to sell the manor house itself. 'If I come with you now it'll save me a journey later on, and I can drive the stakes where you want them. They'll be easy enough to pull up later, when you want to come away.'

So he did not intend to wait for her. Probably he wanted to be back so that he could have the evening free to spend with Eve. There was no reason why she should resent the thought, but she did, and she shook her head, refusing a second cup of tea.

'I'll go and get my sketching pencils.'

She felt breathless, and wanted to get out of the room—away from Ross—to be by herself for a moment or two, to still hands that should not now be trembling, but nevertheless found difficulty in holding the pencils she sought so that she fumbled and dropped them, and had to search under her dressing table until she found the final one that had inconsiderately rolled into a corner and refused to be picked up. At least there's no dust under Amy's furniture, she thought, with a smile that was a travesty of her normal cheerfulness, and nearly dropped it again as Ross's voice floated up the stairs and through her open bedroom door.

'Ready, Katie?'

'Coming!' She grabbed the escaping pencil hastily and hurried through her door, down the stairs to where Ross waited for her in the hall, watching her descend with eyes that she wished he would direct elsewhere. Inexplicably she found his glance disconcerting, and bent to scoop Quiz into her arms to escape their quizzical look before she realised she still had not got her sketching paper.

'I've got it, I'll carry it for you, going,' Ross offered. 'You hold on to this,' he handed her the roll of twine with the loop on the end. 'You can let him run free on the way out, there's no stock at the moment in the fields we'll be passing through.'

'What about ponies?' Katie did not want a repeat of Quiz's earlier performance among them, it might not have such a happy outcome.

'Eve doesn't have any riding lessons to take until this evening,' he said indifferently, 'so there'll be no ponies there, either.'

Evidently they were not going out together. Katie found her earlier theory ill founded, although Ross might well be helping her with the riding lessons, she realised. He seemed fond of children—certainly he made a fuss of the pigtailed Emma whenever she appeared and no doubt he would enjoy the work so long as it kept him in close proxmiity to Eve. They could have all the privacy they wanted when he walked her home afterwards, she thought, and wondered why she should begrudge them this. It was a natural enough wish for any courting couple, to be on their own, so there was no reason why the thought should rankle as it did.

It made her a silent companion as she stepped out beside him, making for the plank bridge across the brook, and the man glanced at her once or twice inquiringly, but finding no response to his casual remarks he walked in silence himself, content to keep his eye on the pup that, now he was with them, seemed intent on exhibiting its best behaviour.

'He comes when you call him,' Katie realised, breaking the silence that she had been too absorbed in her own thoughts to know had caused her companion to wonder.

'He recognises authority,' Ross replied smugly, and Katie looked up at him quickly, catching the familiar glint in his eye that normally would have roused her to battle back, but now she ignored, latching on to the

148

implications of his remark rather than the words themselves.

'The terrier that—came with us, this morning—' she swallowed hastily.

'—Was well trained,' Ross agreed seriously, following her line of thinking. 'It pays,' he added, gesturing towards his own dog that made a chocolate brown shadow at his heels. 'I couldn't keep Glen with me as I do unless I could rely on him to do as he's told. Wait a moment,' he digressed, 'it looks as if the children have moved the plank again. They never think to put it back,' he grumbled, good humouredly, stooping to move the makeshift bridge back to more secure moorings. He pushed asided a patch of waterweed, white with blossom, and Katie watched him dreamily.

'It looks almost solid.' The delicate, floating plant made large rafts that almost covered the brook at this point. 'Quiz, come back!' The pup evidently thought it could be walked upon, and trotted confidently to the edge of the bank where it overhung a patch of the weed, stepping off the side with complete unconcern.

'Let him go.' Ross viewed the inevitable splash philosophcially. 'A ducking will teach him quicker than any amount of scoldings,' he laughed.

'He'll drown!' Katie dashed to the edge of the bank and reach over, and found herself

149

grabbed by a restraining hand.

'Don't you fall in as well, use the plank, it's safer.' He held her to him, and she struggled frantically to free herself. 'Fetch him, Glen,' he added, and there was another splash, a bigger one this time that Katie hardly heard as she hammered her clenched fists against Ross's unrelenting arms, desperate for him to release her until she saw the big crossbred dog paddle calmly out of the water on the other side with the pup caught by its scruff in its powerful jaws. Glen dropped the protesting pup safely on to dry land, its baby fur clinging with wetness to its sides so that the skin showed pink underneath. 'He's not harmed, Katie,' Ross's voice reassured her that her eyes were not deceiving her, and she laughed, shakily, acknowledging the sense of his added, 'Next time, he'll know better than to try and step on waterweed!'

'He's got a headdress of it!' She smiled at the pup's efforts to free itself of the clinging garland, that made it look ridiculously like an Easter bride.

'Let's go and join him on the other side before he tries to get back to us, and falls in again,' Ross laughed, and now he released her, loosing his arms from about her, that she herself had tried to loosen only moments before, and now, contrarily, felt she would give anything if he would let them remain where they were.

CHAPTER SEVEN

'Find yourself a good spot and I'll stake the pup out so that he can reach you if he wants to.' Ross was sensitive to its young need for occasional reassurance when its curiosity proved its undoing.

'Here, under the chestnut tree, would be nice.' The bole would provide a comfortable rest for Katie's back while she sketched, and the massed spikes of white blossom towering above her into the warm air made a ceiling bower of beauty whose walls were provided by a tangle of rhododendrons and lilac, brightened by occasional yellow patches of golden chain, whose delicate blossoms swayed like enormous catkins in the slight breeze. She wriggled herself in a comfortable position, and found a handy tree root that acted as a footrest so that it raised her knees as a suitable angle to hold her sketching board. 'This is ideal!' She sought refuge from her bewildered feelings in the familiar, every day feel of her accustomed work, grasping her pencils and the sketching board—the board Ross had so carefully prepared for her—as if they were anchors in a world that had suddenly become disturbed and insecure, for reasons which she did not feel she wanted to analyse. 'I can see the thatcher at work from here, it's a good point to sketch from.'

'I thought you wanted to do a portrait of him,' Ross reminded her.

'I do, but I'll have to ask him first if he minds,' Katie pointed out. 'And if I'm to do a series of drawings or paintings suitable for the publisher I mentioned, I shall have to include one or two general pictures as well. A thatcher at work would make an ideal one, and an unusual one too, these days.'

'If you like I'll ask the man for you.' Ross hammered the second stake into the ground close to where Katie sat. 'There, that'll keep you out of mischief,' he fastened the cord to the pup's halter and let it loose. 'I've got to have a word with the thatcher anyhow,' he indicated the man still busily at work laying yelms of material on the roof slats that gleamed their newness in place of the charred remains that had been all that were left when she had seen the roof before. 'He'll have to come down for some more reed soon, and I want to have a word with him before I go and see my farm manager.'

'I thought he was using straw.' Katie eyed the material on the roof with an interested eye.

'Straw doesn't give such good wear,' Ross said practically. 'That's the best Norfolk reed, it'll last a good fifty years.' He gazed at his new roof speculatively.

'Goodness! You'll be nearly eighty before

you need to renew it again.' Katie's teeth glinted in a smile, and she tipped her head back to look at him curiously. 'Do you mind about—' She did not know quite how to finish, whether he might think it an impertinence on her part. 'About—all this,' she compromised, and waved her hand vaguely towards the Lodge and the surrounding acres of land.

'About losing the manor house, you mean?' As usual Ross latched on to her train of thought without difficulty.

'Mmm.' She half wished she had not asked, now, but he didn't seem to mind.

'It probably sounds odd to you.' He thrust his hands deep into his trousers pockets, and leaned back against the trunk of the tree so that he was beside her, but still towered above her, so that she had to look up if she wanted to watch his face as he spoke. 'In a way, having to sell the manor house gave me a sense of . . .' He paused, searching for words.

'Release?' Katie suggested quietly, and he glanced down at her in a surprised sort of way.

'You sound as if you know . . .'

'I don't really, at least not in quite the same way,' she replied just as quietly. 'But Mallets has always seemed like a black cloud hovering over my own family.' She hesitated, not knowing how much of her family history Ross knew, but he nodded understandingly.

'You *do* know,' he realised. 'Foolish of me not to have thought of that. But your grandfather did the right thing in the end,' he pointed out. 'Mallets will remain in your family.'

'Yes, I know, but I'm still glad that Mark and I bear a different name.' Somehow she found she could talk to Ross like this, about a deeply felt, personal thing that she would hesitate to even mention to any of her closest friends. 'It'll seem like a new beginning.'

'That's what I felt,' Ross confessed, straightening up from the trunk as the busy thatcher began to beat the last layer of reed under the wooden spar before descending his ladder for a further supply. 'It can be a stifling thing to inherit the accumulations of other people's lives, instead of starting afresh on one's own. Oh, I kept the close family things, the bits and pieces that my parents treasured, and for that reason so do I. And there were some lovely pieces of furniture and china, and so on. That sort of thing,' he said vaguely. So he could be sentimental, too. Katie warmed to the thought. She liked a man who was strong enough to admit to a soft side to his nature, now and then. Only in a general way, of course, she qualified to herself; she didn't like Ross, but that was beside the point. 'I kept the land,' he was saying, in a tone that revealed where his own real interest lay. 'And when the death duties were paid off, there was enough money left to add to it.'

He had added the fields that her grandfather sold. Part of Mallets. A part that should have belonged to her brother, and now did not because they belonged to Ross. Illogical resentment flared in her at the thought. She knew it was illogical, her grandfather had the right to sell what land he chose, but nevertheless she stiffened, and dropped her eyes to her sketching block, beginning the first tentative lines that gave her the outline of the roof.

'Your man's reached ground level.' She wished Ross would go, but after he had taken the trouble to drive the stakes in for her to keep Quiz safely anchored, and also made her the board she held in her hands now, she could not very well be rude, despite the nagging anger that she felt towards him, that she had felt when he first introduced her to Amy, and spoke as if he himself were one of the family, and that now made her want to shout at him that he had no right to the fields that lay on his side of the Burley Brook, the fields that should by rights belong to Mallets, and reason told her now belonged to Ross, since he had paid for them, and there was nothing that either she or Mark could do about it.

'They really belong to Mark.'

She had not meant to let her resentment

155

show; did not, indeed, realise she had spoken out loud until Ross paused, and turned back, his face darkly flushed, and tightening with an expression which she had come to know so well.

'No, Katie, they do not.' His voice was low, tautly controlled, but hard as the steely glint in his eye. 'The land on this side of the brook belongs to me. I have the bill of sale, and if Mark wants it back he will have to buy it from me. *If* I want to sell.' His emphasis on the if told her that in all probability he would not want to. 'And may I remind you,' his tone bit, betraying the depth of his anger that matched her own, 'may I remind you that any transaction of that nature will be between your brother and me. Mallets is no concern whatever of yours.'

He turned on his heel and strode away, and the pup trotted after him until the restraining cord snagged it to a halt, whereupon it sat down with a yelp of frustration that halted the swift, angry movement and brought Ross's hand down to tousle its small head in friendly consolation, but he did not look back, merely resuming his walk in the direction of the thatcher who had seen him coming, and now waited for him beside the bundles of reed on the ground.

Katie glared after him, her own eyes stormy. How dare he speak to her like that!—implying, even if he had not said so in so many words, that she should mind her own business. Mallets was her business. Or at least, it was Mark's, and he had expressly asked her to look after it for him until he was able to come over and attend to it himself. And what had she found? she had asked herself, fuming. A conspiracy between Ross and the solicitor who was supposed to be acting in her brother's interests, to keep her from having any real influence whatever on the running of the farm. Perhaps that was how Ross had obtained his extra land, she thought hotly. Maybe between them, the solicitor and Ross had persuaded her grandfather to sell the acres beyond the brook. It would be easy to persuade a helpless old man . . .

The absurdity of the thought steadied the train of her own. Whatever else her grandfather might have been, a helpless old man was the last description, reason told her, that could have been applied to him. And as for anyone persuading him to do anything he did not want to do, the very idea was ridiculous. Intractable stubbornness was an inborn instinct with Garfield Spurr, and it was more than likely that Ross had bought the land as a favour to an elderly neighbour when the old man found his holding was too much to look after on his own.

Katie shook herself angrily, and wished for the thousandth time that Mark had been able

157

to come and claim his inheritance himself. She wished she could go back to her own work, and what seemed more important just now, return to the peace of mind that was the invariable reward of the total concentration her painting demanded.

'I feel just like you, ruffled all over,' she told Quiz ruefully, stroking his puppy fur flat, an effect which he promptly ruined by shaking it into spikes again, and trotting off on another tour of this new neighbourhood. With a sigh Katie pulled the top sheet of paper from her block, screwing it up in a ball with a quick, impatient gesture that was an unjust slander on the neatly executed outline of the thatcher at work on the half completed roof in front of her. With a frown she bent her attention to the paper, forcing all other matters from her mind, and if she could not quite succeed in quietening the emotions that did not acknowledge the right of her mind to guide them, she put it down to the upsetting experience of the morning, and the open brush she had just had with Ross, which she had so far tried to avoid for her brother's sake.

'The man's impossible!' She dismissed him firmly, allowing her pencil to take control with swift, sure strokes, their speed still dictated by a burning irritation that despite her determination she could not quite subdue. Heavy, dark lines emphasised the strength of the face in her portrait, contrasting with the soft shadows cast by her skilfully guided lead that drew in the straight, rather arrogant nose, and the eyes that looked back at her from the paper, half narrowed with the habitual gaze of one who sees across long distances, to uninterrupted views. They did not seem to look at her, but through and beyond her, and she concentrated on the mouth, on the firm drawn lips above a jawline of uncompromising squareness.

'Heavens! Do I really look as bad tempered as that?'

She had not heard Ross approach across the soft turf, her head bent to her work with absorbed attention, so that she started when his shadow fell across her page, and gazed incredulously at her own drawing, a stern but expressive likeness of the face now softening into a smile above her. What on earth had made her sketch Ross? Mortification stained her cheeks as his teeth glinted in a silent laugh above her head, and she hurriedly slipped one finger under the edge of the paper, intending to treat it as she had treated her first sketch, that still lay in a crumpled ball beside her.

'Naughty! Naughty!' He reached down and deliberately removed the paper from between her fingers. 'That's no way to treat a very good sketch—or its subject,' he added reprovingly, in the tolerant tone he would have used to a fractious child, she thought furiously, and bit her lip to restrain her own retort. 'I did ask you to do a painting for me,' he went on reflectively, 'and since you don't seem to want this, it'll do instead—for the moment,' he said, coolly rolling the paper and slipping the resultant spill into his top pocket with a care that told her he intended it to remain uncreased, though for what purpose he might want the sketch only he could tell, she thought crossly. Vanity, most likely. Katie ignored his offer of a helping hand and sprang to her feet, brushing herself free of twigs and grass that clung to her clothing, and provided her with an adequate excuse not to meet his look. 'And if Mark wants his fields back when he finally takes over Mallets,' Ross added in an even tone to her back, 'he can have them with my blessing. Only Mark will have to ask for them himself, not you,' he told her. 'That way I would know he genuinely wanted them.'

As he wanted her sketch, no doubt. The spill of paper was in his pocket when they returned to Mallets, but it had disappeared when Ross came down to dinner that night, and she refused to ask what he had done with it, deliberately keeping the desultory conversation over their meal on impersonal subjects, and retiring early to bed, using tiredness after their morning walk as an excuse that she fancied he disbelieved, and did not care, she told herself, whether he thought she was telling the truth or not. For all she cared he could use the spill of paper that was her sketch as a taper to light the fire with, she decided, pausing by the wicket gate in the garden wall the next morning to watch Ross and Ben struggle with half a dozen skittish calves in the yard beyond.

'Grab it, Eve!' Ross shouted as one of the young animals dived towards the five-barred gate through which she was just passing, intent on reaching the freedom of the field beyond.

'Back you go!' Imperturbably, Eve grabbed the calf and turned it back into the yard, where it joined its companions in a series of bucks that brought a smile to Katie's face as she watched it.

'Come and help us round them up, Katie. We could do with someone fielding on that side,' Ross called to her, half serious half teasing, and Eve looked round, noticing her for the first time.

'Don't bother if you're afraid, I'll stay and help,' she offered disdainfully, and made her way towards where the men had managed to get four of the calves into a reasonably docile bunch in the centre of the yard.

'Afraid of calves? Don't be silly.' Katie slipped through the wicket gate without pausing to think, anger driving her at the other girl's unpleasantness so that she was

161

able to hide her trepidation from the others if not from herself. If the calf that was nearest to her started to buck like its companion, she would not have the faintest idea how to get hold of it, but now she was committed she would have to try. She gritted her teeth and advanced, and the mischievous little animal eyed her warily. Without warning it spun round to face her, and instinctively Katie sidestepped. In a flash the calf was past her, but this time the gate into the field was firmly closed, and although Ross's exasperated cry of 'Hold it, Katie!' fell on temporarily deaf ears, it still could not escape from the confines of the yard.

'Why on earth didn't you grab it as it went past?' Ross trotted past her in the wake of the calf. He looked hot on the verge of getting cross, and Katie bit her lip, deeming it wiser to hide the grin that he must have read in her eyes, because he scowled, and shooed the refugee back towards its companions with wide flapping arms.

'She was afraid—I told you.' Eve's contempt stung, and Katie flushed, her grin fading.

'Come and hold this one for me,' Miss Katie, he's quiet enough, and I can go and help gaffer get the other two, then.' Ben spoke up quickly across Eve's unfriendly comment, and Katie made her way towards him, willing her reluctant steps to make haste before she justified the other girl's give and brought similar criticism from Ross down on her head. If only she had stayed in the house another ten minutes this wouldn't have happened. But she hadn't, so it was no good wishing, and the calf that Ben held looked docile enough. It was the smallest of the six, and for ease of holding Ben had slipped a rope loop about its neck, the end of which he handed to her.

'There, this one's gentle enough now, just stand still and he'll stay with you—no trouble.' Ben's voice was quietly understanding, and Katie smiled at him gratefully, wondering how she had misunderstood him when she first came to Mallets. Once he had got over his initial shyness he had taken her under his wing and often stopped to explain something or other about the farm that she found new and interesting. The basket that he had brought her for Quiz had been only the first of many such thoughtful things he had done, and she warmed to him now, feeling him to be her only friendly contact in a yard full of bovine delinquents and human critics.

'Take him, Gaffer,' Ben's voice called across the yard triumphantly, 'I've got this one.' Katie turned to see the two men, each escorting a calf that now looked as if butter wouldn't melt in their mouths, back to where she and Eve stood with the others. Eve, too, had slipped ropes round their necks, somehow managing to cope with all three at once Katie marvelled at the ease with which she did it, and tried not to envy her the skill, but reflected truthfully enough that the other girl probably wouldn't know which end of a paint brush was which. The thought brought her own ego back to a more normal level, and made the unfriendly silence from her companion more easily bearable. One of the three animals that Eve held was still restless, shifting about, but held firmly by its neck rope, and as Ben neared them he called out quickly.

'Turn that 'un, Miss Clements. Don't stand behind that calf, Miss Katie...'

His call was ignored by Eve, and not understood by Katie, and by the time realisation hit her it was too late. The calf's tail rose, and it ejected a stream of evil-smelling fluid over Katie's clean denims and shoes.

'Ugh!' She loosed the head-rope of her own calf, backstepped and slipped on the wet cobbles, and landed on her back on the yard, to the tinkle of Eve's amused laughter, and an angry growl from Ben.

'You must have known what that 'un was about, Miss Clements. Why didn't you turn 'un, like I said?' He stopped to help Katie up, but Ross was before him, and his laughter grated even worse than Eve's.

'It's not funny!' She gained her feet and raised her face furiously to his, her eyes snapping.

'I think it is,' he grinned unrepentantly, and kept hold of her, but at arms' length. 'Come on, quick march,' he forced her into action, still keeping her well away from him. 'It's a good job you're down wind,' he chuckled, 'but we'll soon remedy that. We can't have you going back to the house in that smelly condition.' Before she realised what he was about to do, he lifted her bodily into the trough under the yard pump, and with an energetic heave or two of the handle he directed a stream of cold water across her luckless trousers and footwear. The water was icy and the shock of it as it hit her legs and feet stung her back to speech.

'Stop it!' she yelled, 'it's freezing—ouch!' as another stream of icy water drenched her. 'Oh, you brute!' She struggled over the sides of the trough and back on to the yard, and he turned her round and inspected her closely. 'Let go of me!' Stung into furious action, she struck at him with her free hand, and he caught it in his own, fielding the blow and laughing down into her blazing eyes.

'You're clean now,' he told her calmly. 'Go in and change before you catch your death of cold.' He acknowledged the temperature of the water that was drawn from a deep well, and Ben had told her never varied in temperature no matter how hot the summer.

'I hate you!' she stormed at him. 'I hate you both!' Her voice shoke, and she twisted her arm free, somehow keeping her balance on her wet footwear.

'Katie . . .'

She ignored his call, and ignominiously ran, seeking by speed to outpace the sound of Eve's derisive laughter, her blurred eyes only just able to make out the position of the wicket gate in the garden wall. Somehow she found it, fumbled and found the catch and pulled it open. Remembered just in time to shut it behind her, it would be the last straw if she let one of the calves gain the forbidden precincts of the garden, and then she was out of earshot of the yard, running up the stairs without even hearing Amy's query, 'Why, whatever's the matter, Miss Katie?' and into the privacy of her bedroom, and the deep blissful comfort of her own bed. The pillow that received her face tactfully muffled the anguish that she poured into it until a violent fit of shivering told her that she would be wiser to obey Ross's injunction and change out of her wet clothes. A sniffly cold now would no doubt delight him and Eve, and the only satisfaction she would have would be to give it to them both, she thought furiously, grabbing at the first thing that came to her hand, a woollen trouser suit in bright pillarbox red. It would just about match her mood, she thought, as she splashed her face back to normality in the washbasin, and slipped into a white sweater, knowing a satisfaction that Eve would look dreadful in scarlet, with her colour hair. The satisfaction did not last for long, but it helped while it did, and she was able to call 'Come in,' in a nearly normal voice when a tentative tap at her door, and Amy's voice, told her she was wanted.

'I wondered if anything was the matter, miss?' Amy peered round the door hesitantly, and beamed as Katie showed a determinedly bright face in her direction, and began applying a light touch of lipstick to match her trouser suit with an air of complete normality that must have been convincing, she thought with a small sigh of relief.

'Oh, I got the legs of my trousers wet, so I came in to change,' she answered casually. 'Now I'm dressed up I might as well go into the village and post a letter I wrote to a publisher last night. He wants a book illustrated,' she told the interested domestic, who bent to take her soaking denims and shoes from the floor.

'I'll take these and put them by the stove.' Amy meant the kitchen range—she still refused to use the gas cooker, despite Katie's coaxing. 'This overall stuff soon dries,' she slandered Katie's neatly tailored denims.

'Will you keep an eye on Quiz for me while

167

I'm out?' Katie did not feel like taking the pup with her. There were one or two things she might as well attend to while she was in the village, she told herself resolutely, her mind seeking reasons for the trip that she was determined not to acknowledge, even to herself, was really flight so that she should not encounter Ross and Eve again that morning. If she did, she would not be responsible for her actions, she told herself. The blow she had impulsively aimed at Ross, and which he had so neatly dodged, would without doubt have contacted Eve's face if the riding mistress had come within touching distance, she thought furiously, hot anger rising in her again as she remembered what the other girl had done—or not done—to prevent the mishap. As an opponent, Eve did not fight by the Queensberry rules, and the spiteful advantage she had taken of her own local knowledge, so to speak, both this morning and at the auction on the day they attended the sale, made Katie longed to box her ears.

'Amy!'

She heard Ross call through the scullery door, and without stopping to do more than grab her bag and the letter to the publisher, she fled downstairs and out of the front door. There was a bus which passed the end of the drive at about this time. She consulted her watch, and promptly took to her heels. If she ran, she would just about be in time. The battered green face of the vehicle appeared round the bend in the lane just before she reached the gate at the drive end, and she signalled the driver frantically, blessing the typically rural lack of haste that made him slow down and wait for her to run the last few yards, and dive panting through the door he opened for her, thus giving her the best of all excuses for ignoring Ross's call of 'Katie!' She saw him appear out of the front door, saw him start to sprint after her down the drive, but mercifully the bus driver did not. With a mechanical grating that set her teeth on edge, the man set his ancient transport rolling and Katie settled back into her seat with a sigh of relief, conscious of Ross slowing to a frustrated halt as they took the next bend, which turned her side of the bus towards him for long enough for her to see the angry look on his face, and his two hands clamped hard and impotently on the top bar of the gate.

He can be as angry as he likes, thought Katie rebelliously, but he can't expect me to take this morning as a joke. While she was in the village, she would call in to see Jeremy Bailey, and ask the solicitor if he could find a means of terminating Eve Clements's lease of the field at Mallets, she decided. This time the other girl had gone too far, and she had no intention of being so treated in her grandfather's house, whatever the solicitor or

Ross might think about her lack of capability so far as running the farm was concerned.

Now that she had come to some sort of decision her anger cooled a little, and she relaxed in her seat, conscious of tiredness born of the stress of fury and emotional upset which, to a normally calm temperament—albeit that of an artist, she thought with a slight smile—can be a shattering experience.

'. . . her with the red hair, I mean.'

Katie became aware that two ladies, similarly village bound, were enjoying a chance-met gossip in the seat behind her. It sounded as if they might be discussing Eve.

'She's set her cap at him for long enough now,' the second voice agreed.

'Fancies being lady of the manor, I suppose.'

'There isn't a manor anymore. She'll have to settle for being lady of the Lodge,' came the laughing rejoinder. 'The end of Fir Tree Lane, please, driver,' the speaker announced her destination, and with patient courtesy the driver pulled up, leaving his seat to help the two ladies depart with what looked like the week's washing crammed into two enormous plastic bags. Katie remembered there was a modern launderette on the edge of the village, and shuffled towards the end of her own seat preparatory to alighting at her stop on the edge of the village green. The whole village seemed to take it for granted that Eve and

Ross would marry one another, she thought, standing back on the grass and waiting for the bus to trundle off before crossing the street to the bow-fronted building that held the solicitor's office. There was no guarantee, of course, that Jeremy Bailey would be in. She had decided to see him on impulse, but he might be too busy; she had not made an appointment. She scowled absentmindedly at the stocks standing like a silent threat on the green beside her, the ones that Ross had declared were purpose-built to hold one of her own ancestors. Her scowl grew blacker, and she turned her back on the instrument of punishment impatiently. She would not find out if Jeremy Bailey could see her by standing here doing nothing. She crossed the street with quick, firm steps and tapped on the door to which a discreet plate was affixed, and made her wants known to the pleasant-faced clerk in the outer office.

'It's Miss Kimberley, isn't it?' Katie warmed to her smiling recognition. Here at last, she was acknowledged as a person, and not merely as a nuisance to be tolerated, humoured, and laughed at. 'Mr Bailey can see you if you've got time to wait, he'll be another fifteen minutes or so.'

'I'll wait,' Katie decided. 'I'll pop along the street and post my letter.' Her spirits lifted as she dropped her missive to the publisher in the box that proclaimed allegiance to Queen

Victoria, and she traced the raised writing on the side with a reflective forefinger. The post box was in excellent condition; property of any kind in the wold country was well tended and made to last. Ross had chosen reed instead of straw to thatch his roof, declaring it to be good for fifty years. He would be old before it needed renewing. And so would his wife. Katie tried to visualise Ross as an old man—white-haired, and perhaps stooping a little, but with the same piercing directness in his blue eyes that she found so disconcerting now. Eve's hair would probably go a horrid pepper and salt colour, she thought maliciously, but the idea gave her scant satisfaction. Oddly, the thought of Eve and Ross growing old together hurt, as did that of Eve being mistress of the Lodge. Katie liked the Lodge. She felt an affection for the funny, cottage loaf look of it. Perhaps watching the thatcher at work on the new roof had given her this sense of sharing in a new beginning with the old house, making it seem like a link between them.

It was a pity that her link with its owner was not amicable, she thought wryly. The sound of Ross's laughter seared through her mind, as his touch had seared her arms when he lifted her into the trough under the pump, callously sharing Eve's hilarity at her predicament. She hated him, she told herself furiously. Eve wasn't worth hating, she simply despised her, but she hated Ross. Whoever it was who said hatred was akin to love did not know what they were talking about, she decided.

Ben hadn't laughed at her. He had been angry, certainly, but he made it plain that it was with Eve, and not with Katie. She wouldn't have minded Ben sluicing her under the pump, he would have helped her to cope sympathetically, not with ribald enjoyment as Ross had done. Nor would he have held her under the pump with a grip that tingled still. By the morning her arms would be as bruised as her pride was now. She consulted her watch. There was still ten minutes to go, and she sat down on the end of the stocks, unwilling to go indoors to wait. The sunshine was too pleasant to leave for the stuffy confines of the solicitor's outer office.

A tradesman's van trundled round the perimeter of the green—the same one, Katie noticed, that had so frightened her when she had been in the Land Rover with Ross. He had laughed at her then, she remembered, mortified still by the thought that she had given him the satisfaction of witnessing her panic. No doubt he had laughed about it later with Eve. Her face burned at the possibility. It would serve Ross right if the trader's van took a different turning one day, and the two collided. No, not that. Someone might be hurt if they did. The thought acted like a cold douche on her mind, evaporating the heat of her anger. Ross might be hurt. She shivered at the possibility, suddenly glad of the firm feel of the wooden stocks under her, for unaccountably her legs felt weak. She looked up as the door of the solicitor's office opened, and the pleasant clerk put her head round, obviously looking to see if she was in sight. Katie put her hand up to indicate that she was ready for her appointment, and stood up cautiously steadying herself for a necessary moment before the need to collect her poise before she saw the solicitor brought fresh strength to her knees. If the thought of Ross collecting a few scratches as a result of his own careless driving can do this to me, she thought scornfully, then the person who said hatred was akin to love probably *did* know what they were talking about after all, she conceded, with an attempt at humour that might have convinced others, but somehow did not succeed in convincing herself.

CHAPTER EIGHT

'Have lunch with me,' Jeremy Bailey invited. 'We can talk for a little longer, then. I've another appointment first thing this afternoon,' he said regretfully, with a flattering look of appreciation at his attractive client that gave her morale a further boost. The solicitor might be elderly, but he still had a zest for living, thought Katie with a twinkle, remembering his schoolboy enjoyment for sweet biscuits, and liking him more than ever. 'It would be a pity to force the issue now,' he continued, leaning back in his chair over the excellent coffee provided by the local hostelry to terminate a delicious meal that Katie felt she had enjoyed more than she had a right to, considering the nature of her errand. The solicitor's invitation had come as a salve to her pride, providing her with the excuse she was looking for to remain away from Mallets at lunch time.

'Miss Marsh will phone and let Amy know you won't be back,' Jeremy Bailey coaxed, and Katic needed no more persuading.

'I'd love to,' she accepted gratefully, and found that under the influence of good food and better wine that she left her companion to choose, a task he performed with a skill that marked him as a gourmet, her ire faded, and instead of pouring out her troubles to her companion as she had fully intended to she confined herself to generalities, merely inquiring how long it would be before Eve was likely to vacate the field which she now rented for her riding school.

'Miss Clements's use of the field automatically ceases as soon as your brother takes possession,' the solicitor replied, and added with a keen look in her direction, 'it would be a pity to force the issue now,' telling Katie without the need of words that he had read into what she had not revealed more even than he might have gleaned from the spoken word. 'I gather your brother will—er—be a week or two longer,' he smiled, and Katie nodded.

'Yes, but I can stay on until he comes.' Doubtless Eve and Ross would like her to get tired of waiting and go, but she had no intention of giving them that satisfaction, she told herself. Somehow she got the feeling that Jeremy Bailey did not want her to leave, and she warmed towards him as she had done towards his friendly clerk.

'I'm starting a series of illustrations for a publisher I know,' she explained. 'It was Mark's idea really,' she admitted frankly, 'but it appealed to me, and it fits this publisher's need at the moment.' She told him of her aim, enlarging when she found he was an interested audience.

'If you're staying over, you'll need a further advance of money.' Her companion grasped at practicalities.

'As a matter of fact I don't,' Katie interrupted him as he pulled a slim silver pencil from his pocket and a small notebook to make an aide-memoire in his usual meticulous manner. 'That's another thing I wanted to see you about. I've had a letter

176

from my bank this week to say that my own money's been transferred, so I can repay you for the loan.' She fumbled for her handbag and brought out the cheque which she had already written.

'It wasn't a loan,' the solicitor demurred, 'it's your own money, my dear,' he pointed out. 'Part of your legacy,' he stressed gently.

'You know I don't want it.' Katie looked at him levelly, no longer hesitant about voicing her feelings to him on this score.

'Are you so bitter about your grandfather?' The elderly man's voice held regret.

'Not any more,' Katie realised suddenly, and felt a sense of relief—almost of release, she thought wonderingly, as if she had put down a burden she never really wanted to carry. 'I don't feel anything about Grandfather any more, except perhaps pity,' she confessed. 'The past's behind us and done with. The future's ours,' she smiled, and wondered why she said ours, for she had no one in mind to share it with. There was Mark and Wyn and the new infant, of course, she thought with an inward smile, they would do well enough for the 'ours'. 'It all seems such a waste of life, somehow, looking back. He kept all the things that didn't matter, and threw love away,' she finished simply.

Was it a family habit? she wondered later. The thought came unbidden, as such thoughts do, as she stood in the empty hall of

Mallets, wondering at the unusual silence.

'Amy?' She tapped on the kitchen door and poked her head through.

'Oh, miss, I'm glad you're back!' Amy struggled to get her arm into the second sleeve of her showerproof. 'Mr Ross asked me to tell you he won't be in to dinner tonight. He's taken Ben to town for the finals of the darts match,' she explained, 'but he said he'll be back to lock up. I'm off to my mother's, so you'll be able to get yourself something light for your dinner instead of cooking for the rest of us,' she smiled. 'You'll be glad to put your feet up and have a read, I expect.' She bustled out, leaving Katie to forage for herself in the pantry, and wondering if Ross was really staying for the darts match or whether he was playing tit for tat because she had not returned at lunch time, and whether he had, in fact, really gone down to the cottage Eve rented in the village. She did not feel angry with him any more, she discovered, just numb, a sort of creeping lethargy that settled on her spirit like a grey blanket.

It's time I did some serious work, she grasped at her usual antidote to depression, and whistling for Quiz to follow her she picked up her sketching block and pencils that she had left on top of her grandfather's desk in the study, and headed out of doors. There was no sign of Eve. It was too early in the afternoon for the riding lessons to begin, for the older children would still be in school, and she struck across the field towards the brook. This time the pup kept close to her heels, wary of another ducking, and she picked him up in her arms as he hesitated at the plank bridge over the water. Mercifully it was in its proper place today, sure sign that the children were not around, and Katie stepped across it, thankful for the firm feel of it under her feet. If she fell in, Ross would not be at hand to rescue her or Quiz, she reflected, and felt annoyed that she should acknowledge such a need; she had stood on her own feet for long enough now, and she was quite capable of looking after herself without his help. If the firm grip of his arms about her had been reassuring, it was only a temporary port in an emergency, anyone else's arms would have done just as well, but the path towards the Lodge seemed empty, even with Quiz running about her feet, and the gate in front of her was stiff to her small hands, so that she gave up and climbed over, leaving the pup to run underneath.

The thatcher had finished the house roof on the one side, and was trimming the unevenness from the edges with his hook with quick, sure strokes that were fascinating to watch. Katie settled herself on the fence, smiling as he raised his hand in greeting from his elevated position. She had discovered that he did not mind an audience, indeed he encouraged her interest, and like Ben at the farm took time to explain what he was doing, more so since Ross had told him of the book she intended to illustrate.

'I won't promise to sit for you while you paint.' He looked doubtful at her request. 'I've a lot to do, yet. Mr Heseltine wants all the thatch renewed while I'm about it. Reckon he wants the place to look extra smart,' he smiled. Doubtless for when he married Eve, Katie thought, but she did not say so out loud. 'You can see how much there is to do still, and there's only me and the boy,' he went on. The 'boy' was his son, and already a grown man, but Katie did not quibble at his description; it was a common failing of parents to regard their children as Peter Pans. Perhaps she would do the same when she had some of her own, she reflected. If she had children, she amended, and wondered wistfully if she ever would. Her eyes fixed dreaming on the reed thatch, seeking faces in the future, a profitless pastime since the only two that sprang to her mind were those of Ross and Eve, and she shook them away from her thoughts impatiently, the dark head and the auburn, and concentrated on the work going on in front of her.

'One, two, three—goodness, you've got four roofs to thatch!' she exclaimed as the man descended his ladder to collect more material. She had not realised before how extensive the Lodge buildings were, and they were all thatched, even the row of outhouses that looked as if they might at some time have been stables and a coach-house. They flanked a large square yard, and stood adjacent to a modern garage, topped in the same material. Even the summer house in the garden had its own straw hat, she thought amusedly.

'And the pump in the yard at the back,' added the thatcher gravely, watching her silent counting with a twinkle. 'And don't forget the gate,' he gestured towards the lych-style entrance distantly visible at the end of the drive. 'Now you can see why I daren't take time off to sit for you while you paint,' he refused her gently.

'A photograph would do.' Katie had an inspiration. 'That would only take a minute, and I've got a colour film in my camera,' she coaxed. 'I can work from that well enough.'

'Take as many photographs as you like,' the craftsman invited generously. 'While you're here,' he suggested, 'why not take a look around, you might see something else that would illustrate well.'

At least she did not lack interested help, thought Katie appreciatively, as she strolled quietly along the path by the house windows. She peered in, but the downstairs rooms were empty, emphasizing their size, for they were built by a generation that had space to spare.

'The furniture's in the stables,' the thatcher confirmed her guess. 'It's too valuable to risk damaging it by overhead work, so Mr Heseltine had it moved.' He gave her the information gravely and with a friendly nod resumed his interrupted ascent of the ladder, whistling quietly to himself as he went.

He's happy, thought Katie enviously. Happy with himself, and his work. Sure of his skill, and the way he wanted to go. She was sure of her skill, but which way did she want to go? Did she always want to be a professional artist? Or would she be content to make her first love—painting—her second, and give prior place to another occupation? Marriage and children? That thought, like her other, had come unbidden, and because it disturbed her, unwanted. She sat down on the broad step of the old house and put her back against the dark, studded door, shuffling to find a comfortable spot to lean on so that the studs did not dig in. It was not difficult, with her slight frame, and she leaned her head back against it gratefully, feeling that sense of peace that emanates from old houses, whose walls have stood through long years of shower and shine, and learned to accept the transience of each. To the lucky ones who are in tune they bestow their benediction, and Katie received it now, feeling the calm seep through her troubled mind, the patient acceptance touch her own heart, so that the turmoil within her was stilled for a while. Her whole being seemed to wait, listening for what the wise old house might impart, willing to accept its silent deliberations where she could not—would not—accept her own, only to find with returning despair that they coincided; that the way she knew she must go, back to her painting and the busy life that until now she had found satisfying, was not the way she wanted to go, but the latter path must be denied her, since it was the one that only her own heart could tread, and it steadfastly refused to take even the first step along the way unless Ross was by her side.

The phone rang as she returned to Mallets. She put her sketch block down on the hall table, her work face upwards, showing several small, beautifully executed sketches that would eventually be worked up into interesting paintings. Despite her devastating self-discovery, or perhaps because of it, she had applied herself to collecting as much material as possible with a single-mindedness of purpose designed to drive all other matters, even her newly discovered love for Ross, right out of her mind. To a certain extent she had succeeded, her work providing her with an anchor to which she clung desperately in the first throes of her emotional storm, so that the light was beginning to change and the thatcher preparing to pack up for the evening before she realised that it was getting late, and Quiz was whining and begging for her attention in a pathetic manner that told her he was hungry.

'What a shame!' She scooped him up in her arms remorsefully, for the first time glancing at her watch. 'Heavens! It's after seven o'clock.'

'Time to call it a day,' the thatcher agreed, with a smiling 'goodnight' as he left Katie to make her solitary way back to her equally solitary dinner, which she might not want, but the pup must, she thought guiltily, fondling the small body that lay warm against her, too tired with his afternoon of exploration even to bother to chew her thumb. She felt grateful for the little terrier's company. An evening mist curled up from the stream, making a cool dampness that struck chill on her face so that she shivered and hurried towards the house, only to find an even worse chill—that of emptiness— when she got there. The phone at least was a sign of life.

'Mallets.' She lifted the receiver and used Ross's form of identification.

'I want Ross.' It was Eve's voice, brusquely demanding, and not bothering to be polite. For a second or two, Katie was taken aback, then . . .

'I don't doubt you do,' she said sweetly, and forgetting her own manners, firmly dropped the receiver back on its rest.

'I shouldn't have done that,' she told Quiz with an unrepentant grin, and headed towards the pantry, feeling considerably better than she had done when she came in. So Ross was not with Eve after all, and obviously the auburn-haired riding mistress did not know where he was. That thought alone gave her a lot of satisfaction as she busied herself mixing some mince with a handful of meal, and moistened it with a drop of milk before putting the dish down on the floor in front of the eager pup. She discovered her own lifting spirits had brought back her appetite. Hoping Amy would not ask her what she had had for her dinner, she descended to basics and fried herself bacon and eggs, which she ate with Amy's weekly woman's magazine propped up against the coffee pot in bohemian comfort. She was in the middle of a column on readers' problems when the phone rang again. It did not help much, reading about other people's difficulties, she discovered, but at least it brought her own into perspective, she thought, wondering why on earth any woman should ask somebody else's advice on whether or not to leave behind four young children in order to go away with a married man who would leave behind three even younger ones, and this in the sacred name of 'love'. She did not wait to read what the advice would be, the phone kept up its insistent calling, but she

185

hoped the magazine would have the courage to tell its wayward reader to do what she must already know to be right, to work to make the marriage she had already had the success it could be, and tell her 'boy-friend'—Katie screwed her face up in distaste—to do the same, accepting the price that is paid by sacrifice to gain the golden reward that was hers for the taking if she could only see ... Katie sighed. Another misguided human being who was throwing love away.

She opened the door and hurried into the hall, reaching for the demanding phone. What if it was Eve again? Her hand paused half way to the receiver, then resolutely travelled the rest of the way and grasped it firmly. I'm quite capable of dealing with that lady, she told herself robustly, and knew that she lied. She could not compete with her where Ross was concerned, for she knew he was already in love with the riding mistress.

'Mallets.'

'It's Ross here.' Katie started violently and nearly dropped the receiver as the subject of her thoughts spoke in her ear as clearly as if he stood beside her.

'Oh!' It did not sound very intelligent, she realised, annoyed with herself for her confusion, but she could think of nothing else to say. The unexpected encounter had completely unnerved her.

'Katie! Are you there? I'm in a callbox, and

I've only got a minute, I've got no more change.'

'Yes, I'm here. What is it?' Katie found her breath and her voice with a supreme effort.

'We've had a puncture on the way back from the darts match. I've got to stop to change the wheel, and I want to take the spare in to Bob Smith on the way back,' he mentioned the local garage proprietor who was accustomed to having work dropped into his shed at the back of his cottage at all sorts of unexpected hours, and cheerfully accepted such commissions ready for when he opened his business the next morning. It would mean a fairly long detour if Ross was taking his usual route back from town, and it told Katie he and Ben were likely to be back fairly late. 'Ask Amy to lock up the stock for me, will you? We shan't be back until after dark now.'

'Amy's gone...'

'What did you say? Oh, there's the pips. I'll have to go,' as the telephone signalled his time was up.

'But, Ross...'

Various mechanical noises told Katie he had not heard her, and she put the receiver down, wondering what she should do. She had no idea where Ross might be ringing from. Why on earth didn't I ask him? she scolded herself for her lack of foresight. I could have rung back then ... But it was useless to reproach herself now, it was too late, and if Ross had no more small change with which to obtain another call he would not be ringing back. She would just have to do the nightly rounds of the farmyard herself. There was no knowing when Amy would be back. She returned to the kitchen and found out the storm lantern that always stood ready filled and primed on a table in the corner. Why on earth doesn't Ross use a powerful torch? she wondered exasperatedly, as she fumbled with the lamp glass, her unaccustomed fingers having to try several times before she found how it lifted off the base, and then she remembered that Ben normally did the locking up, and stubbornly stuck to the old-fashioned method of lighting his way round the yard. Ben and Amy made an excellent pair in this respect, thought Katie ruefully, the one with his light and the other with her stove, and prophesied a radical change when Mark arrived. Her brother, she had no doubt, would install electric light in the outhouses, and if he could not get it from the mains she felt sure he would find some means to generate his own. Mark loved light with almost the veneration of a painter, and while he revered the good things from the past, he never slavishly followed them simply because they were old, believing it to be better to discard obsolete ways and use new ones where they were proven to be better. He held a similar outlook to Ross, in a way, thought Katie; the two should make amicable neighbours.

There was no help for it. She lit the lamp resolutely, glanced quickly round the kitchen to make sure there was no obvious mischief the pup could get into while she was out, and closed the door behind her. She need not worry about Quiz, she thought with a smile; the combined effects of an afternoon exploring the garden of the Lodge, and a hearty meal to finish off with—he had wolfed every scrap she had put down for him, and clattered his dish across the kitchen floor while making certain there was no crumb left undiscovered underneath—had had the effect of reducing him to blissful unconsciousness on the hearthrug in front of the low fire, with only a twitch or two of his small limbs and an occasional whimper, to betray the excitement of his rabbit-chasing dreams.

The farmyard outside seemed dark and eerily empty after the cosy, lighted room. Katie heard the kitchen clock strike ten as she shut the door behind her. She must have been reading Amy's magazine for longer than she had realised. She swung her light above the coops containing the fowl, checked the fastenings, and found them intact, and she picked her way across the yard suddenly wishing she had brought the pup with her for company. An owl called from close by, making her jump nervously, and then the

189

pale form of the big bird drifted across the rickyard, coasting on slow, powerful wings, hunting for rats or mice for its supper. Katie tensed, listening for the shrill squeak that would tell her it had killed, but none came, and she did not know whether to feel glad for the rodent population or sorry for the owl, that called again, farther away this time, and still hunting.

A quick patter of feet stopped her own in mid-stride, and she held her light higher, her heart pounding.

'Oh, it's you.' She turned towards the billygoat, unexpectedly glad of its company. It was still in its railed enclosure, but according to Ross it was ready to be put out among the sheep.

'You've tamed him?' she asked incredulously when Ross mentioned what he intended to do.

'Oh, yes, he's gentle enough now. In fact he comes up to me of his own accord whenever I'm in the yard,' he retorted smugly. 'Scratch his head if you go near his pen, it all helps public relations,' he grinned, but she refused to be drawn by his teasing, determined not to give him yet another excuse for amusement at her expense.

'I wonder ...' she murmured to herself. She reached out a tentative finger, and the goat raised its head expectantly, its eyes mild in the soft light from the lamp. Katie touched it gingerly, and when it still stood without movement she rubbed its poll, to the animal's evident enjoyment. 'My word, Ross was right,' she acknowledged, with awe in her voice.

'I'm quite good at taming—things,' he had boasted facetiously the day before, and she had glared at him angrily, reading the meaning behind his deliberate pause, and resenting it as applied to herself. Or maybe he had meant Eve. From a man's point of view Eve would probably be worth trying to tame; she had a fiery temperament that did full justice to the colour of her hair, and doubtless it would represent a challenge to the man who sought her hand, Katie thought, realism forcing her to acknowledge the attractions of her rival. Except that Eve wasn't even a rival. Ross's affections were already won, and he had never looked on Katie as anything more than a necessary nuisance.

'My mood's as black as your coat,' she told the contented goat, that watched her depart with blank-looking yellow eyes that made Katie wonder what thoughts went on in its head.

She dutifully toured the line of byres, shutting the top doors and sliding the locks into place until there was only the bull's pen left to cope with. She turned towards its stall, which she knew Ross usually liked to shut up last of all; she had come out with him on a similar errand several times since she had been here, while Ben was in the throes of his darts tournament, and she was familiar enough by now with the routine. The top half of the double door had to be shut across and bolted, like the other byres, but she remembered Ross usually slid the hatch of the fowl coop to the floor as well, so that its occupants would not disport themselves about the stable before Ben came to let the bull out in the morning. She smiled at the thought of so huge an animal liking a pen of fowl for company, but she supposed even bulls could be lonely. A bond of fellow feeling made her think of the bull more kindly; she was feeling lonely enough herself, in all conscience, as well as dispirited.

She hurried, realising she was a lot later than the usual time of the nightly round, and when she looked over the door she saw that the bull was already lying down with its back to her on the thick pad of straw bedding. That probably felt supremely comfortable to the animal, she thought, raising her lamp high so that she could see clearly to unbolt the bottom half of the door and let herself in. She slipped inside quietly, unwilling to disturb the sleeping animal, for despite her fellow feeling she was still nervous, and she turned to rebolt the door, a precaution that Ross never missed. He would never allow her to live it down if Buttercup trotted out into the yard and she could not get him to go back by the time the men returned. She still held the lamp at arm's length above her head, and disturbed by the light, the bull awoke and started to get to its feet, coming to its knees in the way bovines do, that convinces sentimentalists that they had disturbed the animals in an attitude of prayer.

As the bull lumbered to its feet Katie paused uncertainly, and the lamp threw a grotesquely misshapen shadow of the beast on the clean, whitewashed wall in front of the bull's face, from the light behind it. For a breathless instant she saw the bull go rigid as the black, heaving mass of shadow climbed the normally blank wall like a ghost, then with a bellow of fright it spun round to face her, its reddened cyes glaring at the intruder. The sight of Katie stopped it short for a brief, breathtaking second, pawing at the stable floor with sharp rasping sounds as its hooves struck through the straw bedding to the quarries underneath. Katie froze with horror as she remembered that in the stable the bull was never chained, but free to move about the pen at will, and it was only a matter of a few short feet from her.

'There's no need to be afraid of him,' Ross had said when she first arrived. 'Cup's gentle enough, animals usually only attack if they're afraid.'

The bull was unmistakably afraid now, and

there was no doubt about its intention to attack. With another ear-shattering bellow, that echoed round the bare walls of the stable with a noise that sounded in Katie's ears like the knell of doom, it charged. She dropped the lamp from nerveless fingers, and jumped. Terror lent her upward propulsion. The beam that ran across the stable several feet above her head would normally be well out of her reach, but her fingers somehow found the rough wood, and regardless of splinters she clung on, drawing her legs up under her just as the bull passed below with only a matter of inches to spare. With an agility she would not have suspected in so bulky a creature it spun and charged again, all the while keeping up the terrible bellowing that took every ounce of strength from Katie's limbs, so that she felt herself slipping, and wondered desperately how long she would be able to cling on. Vague memories of gym lessons during her schooldays prodded at her mind, and in the brief seconds available before the bull turned again in the confined space at its disposal she swung her legs high, curling them across the top of the beam, one on each side, with a desperate clinging that took some of the weight of her body from her over-strained arms. It left her suspended upside down, and the bull reached up, pawing, only just missing the curve of her back. She was thankful that she was dressed in trousers; if she had been in a skirt that hung down . . .

Somehow, she realised, she would have to heave herself up on to the top beam if she was to stay whole. With muscles long unaccustomed to such strenuous exercise she inched her way upwards, her need to reach the top of the beam driving her protesting body to the only haven of safety available in the whole of the stable. A splinter dug in, but she gritted her teeth and ignored it—time enough to worry about splinters when this was over, even if she had to have them lanced out, she thought stoically. One last effort, that left her gasping for breath and trembling all over, found her lying on the top of the narrow beam, clinging to its reassuring hardness with a limpet grip. She mustn't faint. If she fainted now, and fell . . . The mere thought of it nearly brought about the condition she feared, and she shook her head savagely, feeling her senses slip away so that her arms and legs loosed their grip, and a hazy blackness penetrated her mind. It was a warm, inviting blackness, that held out its folds to her, tempting her to succumb and forget everything, the bull, Ross and Eve, and the whole miserable burden that she now carried with her since her moment of revelation beside the Lodge—Ross's home—that afternoon.

Cluck—cluck!

The homely sound saved her. The very

unexpectedness of it, cutting across the maddened screaming of the bull and the pounding of her own heart that seemed as if it would deafen her with the thudding of the blood against her eardrums, brought her back to full consciousness, and she looked down. One of the hens, with the strutting curiosity of barnyard fowl all over the world, had clucked itself into the arena to see what was going on. It turned a haughty look on its mountainous stable companion and clucked again, and an hysterical laugh rose in Katie's throat. It sounded just like her old governess when she had transgressed one of the schoolroom rules. The bull heard it too, and Katie shuddered and felt sick as it spun on the small feathered thing, and its companions that were beginning to cluck and stir inside the coop. With a silence that was even more terrifying than the previous bellows, it jumped on the coop, deliberately stamping the unfortunate occupants into a mass of pulpy feathers, mingled with splinters that were all it left of the once stout coop. With a squawk of fright the first hen took wing, and landed on Katie. She jumped convulsively, and it took off again, landing further along the beam, and Katie pushed herself to a sitting position cautiously, reaching back for a wooden upright to the roof that would do as an added support. What a time to find out I don't like heights! she thought shakily. The upright was a good foot behind her, and holding her breath she began to shuffle backwards. An inch, two, and she came to a halt, a nail in the beam snagging her trousers. Let them tear, she thought grimly; she'd have no need of a trouser suit if she fell now, and the bright cherry colour of the cloth would be stained a deeper shade. She shuddered, concentrating every ounce of energy on reaching the upright. The feel of it against her back was like reaching harbour after riding a hurricane, and she relaxed briefly, allowing some of the trembling in her body to still while she decided what to do.

The bull was still giving vent to ear-splitting roars that must be alerting the countryside for miles around, she thought hopefully, wondering how long it would be before anyone heard and came to see what was amiss. Then she remembered that Ross's house was Mallet's nearest neighbour, and that was empty. Unless someone happened to be travelling late along the lane that ran beyond the farm drive, she would have to wait for Ross and Ben. She would hear their vehicle come up the drive, she comforted herself, she could shout loud enough to warn them, and surely Ross would know what to do. It was impossible for her to reach the stable door. She could not even swing herself across the top opening, the beam was a couple of feet out of line of the door itself, and it would need the agility of a circus performer to stage such a feat. Mercifully it was not entirely dark in the stable. She looked for the lamp, and gasped with horror. It lay on its side, paraffin seeping from the bottom in a slow spreading wetness along the floor. It had not reached the straw yet, but if it did ... Her mind froze at the thought. If it set light to the stable, both she and the bull would surely die.

'Katie! Katie, where are you?'

It was Ross's voice.

'Miss Katie?' Ben joined in the chorus, and from somewhere behind them Katie could hear Amy's treble alarm shouting her name.

'I'm in here. Ross, be careful!' as running footsteps sounded on the stable yard, and skidded to a halt by the stable door. 'Watch out!' The bull, hearing what it must have taken to be further intruders threatening its safety, rammed the door with the full weight of its bulk behind the blow. The planks sagged, but held, and Ross's face, chalk white in the light of the powerful torch he held in his hand, described a circle, peering for her whereabouts in the gloom.

'I'm up here, on the beam.' Somehow she found her voice to explain. 'I'm quite safe, but the lamp ... It's all right, that's safe now, too,' she choked suddenly, her body wet with perspiration that was a measure of her dread as the bull, unable to find a human victim, and having disposed of all the trapped fowl, except one, turned on the lamp and trampled that, too, into a twisted mass of metal. 'The flame's gone out,' she breathed, unable to believe her own good fortune.

'How long can you sit it out?' Ross's voice, taut with anxiety, penetrated through the gloom in the intervals between the bull's roars. 'Are you hurt?'

'No, I'm fine. It's very uncomfortable up here, though. And cold,' she realised, shivering, the perspiration of her earlier fear suddenly turning on her in a clammy embrace.

'Never mind the cold, and be thankful you're uncomfortable,' Ross said curtly. 'That way, you're not likely to go to sleep.'

'Sleep? While I'm up here?' Katie called back incredulously.

'You might well be up there all night,' Ross retorted grimly. 'You can't swing down through the door from the beam, it's too far away to be safe, and you can't come down any other way until Cup's calmed down,' he said practically, the very sense of his utterance bringing a measure of reassurance to Katie. 'I can keep him from charging about with this.' A slender, pronged tool appeared through the door, and peering down Katie discerned the business end of a pitchfork, that normally peaceful maker of hay that now took on a new and ominous use.

'He's going to charge again. Ross, get away from the door...'

'He won't face this.' Ross stood his ground confidently, and Katie shut her eyes, then opened them again hurriedly. She daren't look, and she daren't not look. The bull started forward, then seeing the gleam of metal it arrested its charge and backed off, pawing the weaving its great head threateningly, but acknowledging the domination of those two steel prongs that remained unwaveringly over the door.

'That's better.' Ross talked quietly, evenly, with no sign of disturbance in his tone. 'Now calm down...'

'I am calm!' Katie snapped, the combined effects of fright and cold having their reaction.

'I'm not talking to you, I'm talking to Buttercup,' Ross threw back at her, and continued to talk quietly, persistently, ignoring the answering roars, until Katie began to wish irritably that at least one of them would be quiet. Her head ached with the constant noise. She leaned back on the strut behind her and shut her eyes. 'Katie! Wake up!' Ross called her, insistently, urgently, and she opened them again.

'I'm not going to sleep.'

'You'd better not,' his voice was grim, 'or you'll end up like that pen of fowl,' he promised her with such obvious truth that

Katie forgot her headache as being something too trivial to worry about.

'What'll happen if he doesn't calm down? I can't stay here indefinitely.'

'You may have to for an hour or two,' Ross said with blunt lack of sympathy that flicked on the raw. 'But he should quieten when it gets daylight,' he said optimistically. 'When he can see all round him again, and there aren't any dark corners, or shadows. Was that what frightened him?' he questioned her.

'I haven't the faintest idea,' she retorted. 'All I know is that I came into the pen to drop the hatch across the end of the fowl coop...'

'And I suppose Cup was asleep, and it never occurred to you to wait for a bit and talk to him, make sure he was awake and knew you were there.'

'W-e-ll, no. I went in quietly so as not to disturb him—it would only take a minute to reach the coop and drop the hatch,' she said defensively. 'The bull must have heard me, because he started to get up.'

'And your lamp was behind him. It would throw his own shadow on the wall right in front of his face,' Ross deduced as clearly as if he had been there, thought Katie wonderingly. 'Think how you'd feel, hearing someone come into your bedroom when you were half asleep, and seeing a great black shadow move across the wall. You'd scream, wouldn't you?'

'Maybe I would, but that won't help me get out of here now,' Katie said crossly. 'What'll you do if he keeps this up all tomorrow?' The bull looked more than capable of doing just that, she thought apprehensively. She had only to move slightly on her insecure perch to bring its great head up, and the reddened eyes fixed on her with an evil intent that sent her cold with fear.

'I'll have to shoot him,' Ross said quietly, and added, 'but I don't want to do that. It would be a criminal waste to destroy a good bull because of a silly woman's witless action.' His tone cut through her like a knife, it even stopped her teeth from chattering for a brief instant that clenched them together in a fury that made her jaws ache. 'So you see, Katie, you'll have to bear with my company for the rest of the night,' he grinned suddenly, his face briefly illuminated by the lamp that Ben carried somewhere out of sight, that shone on his gleaming teeth, but mercifully did not penetrate the interior of the stable far enough to show him Katie's burning face.

CHAPTER NINE

He makes it sound as if we're sleeping together, she thought furiously. Oh, I hate you! she breathed, ignoring her discovery of that afternoon, even welcoming the returning fury that possessed her, because it helped her to forget that other, overwhelming feeling that try as she would to stifle it, still lurked like a dark shadow in the background.

Love should not be like this, she thought miserably, easing herself to a more comfortable position on the beam, if that was possible on so hard and narrow a surface, to say nothing of the splinters ... Surely love should be a peaceful, happy feeling, like the first welcome rays of warm sunshine after a hard winter, unfolding like the cautious petals of the first shy flowers to defy the bleak weather. Her love was bringing her nothing but unhappiness. No, that was not the fault of her love. She considered her dilemma with the clear detachment that sitting on a beam a few feet above instant death could bring to a person. It gave her time to think, and in a way the constant uproar below her gave her a kind of privacy, an isolation that rendered her immune from the petty affairs of the world, wrapped in a cocoon that allowed her to analyse her feelings with a ruthless honesty, while her acute physical danger anaesthetised her from mental pain. Almost. Ross's face, occasionally illumined as Ben moved restlessly from one foot to the other, his fidgeting swinging his lamp so that the soft light fell on the lean outline of Ross's jaw, had the power to bring a sharp stab of anguish in the region of her heart, but that did not prevent her from watching for those brief, infrequent glimpses, safe in the knowledge that Ross could not see her own face at all clearly; in the gloom of the stable roof she would be little more than a blurred outline to him.

So she waited and watched, wishing Ben would swing his lamp towards Ross more often, becoming impatient when Ben or Amy spoke to her and disturbed her privacy—Ross was concentrating on talking to the bull; he probably preferred it to talking to her, Katie thought gloomily. Gradually Ben's light grew dimmer. He's probably running out of paraffin, she thought, and hard on the heels of her wondering if he had noticed his lamp was fading came the realisation that it was gradually growing light. The first noisy scolding of a blackbird diminished quickly to a sleepy murmur somewhere close by, as if it had landed on the roof of the stable, having found its first exuberant efforts too much so soon after waking, and a faint grey light penetrated the stable, so that Ross's head and shoulders became clearly visible. He still held the pitchfork in front of him, warily cautious, knowing better than to put foolish trust in any animal, but leaning with his arm bent across the stable door, outwardly relaxed, and still talking, gently, quietly, his voice a persistent murmur that had now taken over in frequency from the bull's roars. Katie turned her head and looked at the bull. Her movement no longer incited it to paw the ground, but it raised its great head, and she realised with a flash of pity that it was probably as weary of the night as she. Carefully she stretched her limbs, cramped almost into paralysis from cold and her hard perch.

'Katie?' She hardly realised that Ross had spoken directly to her.

'I'm still here!' she retorted, unable to resist the bite in her voice when she grasped the fact that he had for the moment ceased talking to the bull and condescended to speak to her.

'We'll soon alter that.' A weary grin crept over his features, and she saw with compunction that he, too, was as tired as she was. Probably he had been more worried even than herself, she thought, he would feel responsible for her while she was at Mallets. He was only in charge of the farm, but being Ross he doubtless felt that he was in charge of her as well. Her thoughts took on the familiar asperity, and she shrugged them away as unjust. He could have left her to sit it out alone. The thought silenced her with its awfulness, and she listened carefully as he spoke again. 'Swing your legs down off the beam, that will get some use into them, and test out Cup's reaction,' he told her quietly.

205

'That's right,' as she let one leg drop slowly, then as the bull still continued to stand, albeit restlessly, she dropped the other, feeling pins and needles ooze up her limbs as the sluggish blood began to flow with excrutiating agony. 'Can you feel your feet yet?'

'Just about,' she answered. 'I reckon I'm mobile,' she hastened to assure him as she caught swift anxiety in his glance.

'Then shuffle along the beam. Go slowly, you've got plenty of time,' he coaxed. 'Don't make any sudden movement, now Cup's quiet I don't want to start him up again,' he said feelingly.

'Neither do I, don't worry!' Katie edged her way inch by inch along the length of the beam towards the door. The last hen, that had spent the night as her companion, took off with a squawk and a flutter, and she froze as it landed on the floor in front of the bull. She heard Ross's sharp intake of breath, and a mutter from Ben in the background that brought a hissed rebuke from his wife, but the bull ignored the hen as being beneath its notice. After a tense minute, Ross spoke again.

'Start shuffling forward again.' He talked in the same even, monotonous tone that he had used on the bull, but Katie was too tensed up to care. When she reached the end of the beam she would have to drop to the ground and cover the few remaining feet to the door before the bull. She could feel the animal watching her, sensing the intentness of its stare, and she kept her eyes resolutely on the opposite wall which was her goal, fearing irrationally that it might hypnotise her into falling if she was to look down and meet its eyes.

'I've gone as far as I can.' The upright to the roof opposite to the one she had been leaning on until now barred her way, and she came to a full stop, undecided what to do next. 'What happens now?' she threw at Ross tautly.

'Sit there and talk to me for a minute or two, until you've calmed down,' he suggested casually.

'I'm calm enough,' she protested, 'and I want to come down. I've had enough of being marooned on this beam all night.' It was all right for the hen, but no place for a human being to sit on for hours on end. She rubbed her nether regions ruefully, and wondered if she would ever sit comfortably again. She glared down at Ross, longing to erase the grin that spread mischievously across his face.

'Just the same, you're edgy,' he said shrewdly. 'Cool down a bit,' he urged her. 'Animals can smell fear, and you're probably sweating.' She was, the palms of her hands were wet, and she rubbed them hastily against the legs of her slacks, giving herself away. Why on earth did I buy this trouser suit? she wondered, regarding the red colour with distaste. I don't think I'll ever wear anything red again. Not that the colour had bothered the bull, it had been too dark for the animal to see whether her suit was red, white or blue, and she didn't believe the old folk tale anyway. Nevertheless it would remind her ... she shuddered as she looked down at the bull's front legs that the growing light showed flecked to the knees where it had trampled on the pen of fowl.

'Think of something nice, it'll take your mind off where you hurt most,' Ross said maliciously. 'It's a pity you don't ride, like Eve. If you were used to a saddle you wouldn't have found it quite so hard up there,' he taunted softly, and she gritted her teeth, willing herself to sit easily and try and look as if she didn't hurt all over by now. Anger made her succeed, and she swung her legs to and fro to keep some feeling in them with an irritated thrust that ignored the bull, making her want only one thing, to get out of earshot of Ross's mocking jibes that made her long to box his ears almost as much as she had wanted to Eve's earlier on.

'I'm coming in.' He stopped her thoughts abruptly, bringing her attention on to what he was doing. With unhurried calm he reached inside the stable door and pulled back the bolt, and Katie saw that Ben was just behind him. Without a word both men slipped inside the stable, and Ross, as he always did, bolted the door behind him. They were all three locked in with the bull! The coolness of their move, made so adroitly that they had completed it before she realised what they intended to do, made her gasp, and she had time to wonder at Ben's agility as he slid behind Ross into the stable as if he was as slender as the man he followed. Then she saw that both men carried pitchforks, the pronged ends of which were pointed remorselessly in the direction of the bull. It grumbled restlessly at this new intrusion, swaying its huge body to and fro on the legs that had always looked too slender to carry it, but that Katie knew now had a steel-like strength of their own, but as the two men stood stock still it settled again and Ross took a cautious step forward until he was directly underneath Katie.

'Don't jump,' he directed her quietly. 'Any sudden movement now would be asking for trouble.'

'Then what...?'

'Just do as I say and everything will be all right.' He sounded so calm, so confident that Katie instantly felt it would be, and hoped she would have the courage to obey whatever he ordered her to do. 'Swing your legs over the beam and stand on my shoulder,' he told her. 'Don't worry, I can take your weight and more.' He gave way to impatience, then quickly checked himself. 'Once your one foot is on my shoulder and you feel steady, tell me.'

'That's it.' Katie eased herself down into what seemed an endless void of space before she felt his shoulder through her soft footwear. 'I'm quite secure,' she assured him.

'Right, then hold on to the beam and steady yourself with your hands,' he answered her quietly. 'I'm going to walk backwards as far as the wall, then along the wall to the door, but I daren't let go of this fork, just in case,' he warned her, 'so I can't use my hands to help you. Do you understand what I want you to do?' he insisted.

'Yes, I'm ready when you are.' How safe she felt now, with only her one foot giving her fragile contact with Ross. How safe to be with him always! She faltered for a hand-hold and brought her thoughts up sharply. This was no time to indulge in daydreams; her own life and those of the two men beneath her might depend on her concentration now.

'Right, I'm going to start walking backwards—now.' He suited action to his words, walking slowly one step at a time, then a pause, never taking his eyes away from the bull, and giving Katie plenty of time to adjust her own position, 'walking' with her hands along the beam, almost imperceptibly drawing further away from the bull and nearer to the door. Once Ross stopped and she felt him go rigid, conveying the strain he laboured under as the bull took a step towards them, swaying its great head threateningly to and fro, but Ben calmly moved forward, pitchfork in hand to reinforce the one Ross held, warning the bull of the folly of another attack, and it desisted, contenting itself with warning rumbles that Katie felt would surely unbalance her precarious hold if they turned to its former ear-shattering roar. She felt rather than heard Ross's sigh of relief, a careful exhalation of breath that preceded his movement, and they were walking towards the door again, inch by careful inch, until Katie longed to scream to him to run, anything to end this awful nerve-stretching perambulation that diced with death or at best dreadful mutilation, their only defence the steel courage of the man who bore her on his shoulder, and the puny-looking pitchforks that from where Katie stood looked about as useful as a baby's rattle against the angry shorthorn.

'We're almost against the wall.' She breathed the words quietly, guiding him. 'I'm balanced against it now,' her hands left the rough wood and found whitewashed brick, cool and smooth after their former hold.

'I'm going to start walking sideways, then,' Ross responded as quietly, and began edging towards the door. It was only a matter of a few feet, but it seemed like miles to Katie before he stopped where the cheerful sunlight streamed in through the open top half. Never had Katie welcomed it so fervently—the sight of the farmyard, and Amy's homely face peering in from a safe distance, seemed more welcome to her than any scenery in the world. 'Can you step on to the bottom half of the door?' Ross backed a step himself so that Katie was right above it.

'Yes.' Tentatively she reached out with her free foot that all this way had dangled over nothing, and felt the wooden spar of the door firm under the sole of her shoe.

'Then swing yourelf on to it, and jump through. Amy will catch you.'

'What about you?' She'd be leaving him and Ben in the stable, and her heart misgave her.

'Do as I say. Quickly,' his voice held urgency as scraping sounds came from the floor. The bull was pawing again. 'Now!'

She released her hold of the wall, grabbed the side post of the door, and with her foot on top to act as a lever, vaulted through the opening and landed safely in the farmyard outside.

Oh, miss . . . !' Amy ran forward, catching at her, and Katie saw with surprise that she had been crying, her cheeks were wet. Of course, Ben was still in the pen with Ross . . . She spun and ran back to the door. Ross evidently expected her, for he spoke immediately.

'He's going to charge again, pitchforks or not ... Slide the bolt away, Katie, and let us through.'

She stood on tiptoe and reached inside, fumbling for the bolt. In her nervous haste she was at first unable to move it, and then it gave, pulling away from its hold and setting the door free.

'Don't swing it wide—just ease it open. Now Ben, you first.' There was no argument. There was no time. Ben simply did as he was told. Among the brave, Katie realised suddenly, there was no time for heroics. The farmhand slid around the front of Ross, still keeping his pitchfork at the ready. He slipped through the opening of the door, and immediately went along the other side of it and leaned through, presenting his weapon.

'Ross ...' Katie caught her breath in her throat, her murmur lost in a bellow from inside the stable. Ross shouted, she didn't hear what he said, and then with the speed of lightning he sprang through the door to her side, turned instantly and slammed it shut, ramming the bolt home, and pulling his arm clear just as the bull's head struck the place where it had been.

'Don't worry, it won't give. They're oak planks, and it'll take more than Buttercup to break through them.' Ross reached out and pulled Katie to him, hearing her quickly

213

stifled sob. 'There's no need to cry.' There was a touch of asperity in his tone that stiffened Katie away from him. 'There's no real harm done,' he pointed out. 'You aren't injured—are you?' He eyed her intently, relaxing as she shook her head. 'And we didn't have to shoot the bull.' He sounded more relieved about that than about her, thought Katie mutinously. 'Now go into the house, Amy will make you a cup of tea. And I suggest you both get to bed for an hour or two, it's been a long night.' His own shoulders sagged a little, with tiredness Katie guessed, and she felt remorseful. It was her fault.

'I'm sorry . . .' she began, feeling somehow an apology was due, though looked at logically there was no real reason for her to apologise. It was a perfectly understandable mishap, done with the good intention of helping Ross and locking the stock up for him before he got home. She could have left them. Miserably she wished she had, but it was too late now. His words had bitten deep. He had called her efforts to help him 'a silly woman's witless action,' and it hurt.

'I'm glad—in a way.' His words were barely audible, and Katie shrank away from him. So he was glad. No doubt it would give him an opportunity to demand that Jeremy Bailey should find her other accommodation. She had been in the way from the time she walked into Mallets, and now here was the perfect excuse to get rid of her.

'Shall I get some breakfast?' Amy grasped at everyday practicalities, and brought them all back to normal. They turned on her with relief.

'Yes, we're all hungry.' Ross spoke in a decided tone. 'Ben and I will finish the stock here now we're out. Have your own meal,' he instructed Amy and Katie with casual impartiality, 'then go and have a sleep. We'll follow you in when we've finished, then you'd better do the same, Ben,' he instructed. 'I'll stay around until mid afternoon, and you can take over from there. We'll have to keep an eye on Cup for the next twenty-four hours or so, to make sure he stays in the right frame of mind. I daren't risk turning him out for a while after this.' He spoke thoughtfully, ignoring Katie and Amy. Evidently he's finished giving us our instructions, thought Katie with a flash of irritability that was born of tiredness and fright, and now he's dismissed us. Slowly she turned after Amy towards the house, realising for the first time how exhausted she felt. It was an effort to put one foot in front of the other, and Amy slowed down and waited for her. With unaccustomed familiarity, she slipped her arm through Katie's, and the two woman walked to the house together, brought close by the events of the night.

'Ben's a brave man.' Katie broke the silence.

'Oh, Ben knew what he was doing. And Mr Ross. They're used to handling animals,' Amy replied calmly, bringing her companion's eyes round to her in surprise.

'But you were crying?'

'That's right, I was,' Amy admitted in her slow way, no whit put out by the accusation. 'You see, I thought you was going to be killed,' she explained. 'If you'd fallen off of that beam, Cup would have had you for sure . . .'

Amy had been crying for her! 'Oh, Amy!' In the seclusion of the kitchen, Katie impulsively threw her arms about the placid domestic, and hugged her.

'There, there,' Amy patted her soothingly on the back, as if she was no bigger than Emma, thought Katie, knowing that she had deeply touched the other woman by her impulsive move. 'Help me put the cups out now.' Amy came nearer to being as gruff as Ben than Katie would have thought possible with a woman's voice. She returned Katie's rather watery smile with a bright beam, and a bond was forged between the two that, Katie thought forlornly, would last a lifetime of friendship if she could only stay. But that was not to be. She fitted cups into saucers, her hands moving automatically about the familiar task.

'I don't want anything to eat.' With her feelings as disturbed as the night itself had been, food was the last thing she felt like.

'Just the same, you must have a bite of something.' Amy was adamant. 'Have some cereal and a bit of toast.' She shook the cornflakes packet sparingly over a dish and coated it liberally with sugar and milk before putting it firmly in front of Katie, and sitting down to her own. Listlessly, Katie complied. It was easier to give in than to argue. 'There's the post.' A thump on the hall mat confirmed Amy's guess.

'It's morning,' Katie realised dully. The start of another day. Her mind had been numb, not grasping the reality that was time, and the fact that other people were going about their daily work unshaken by the shattering experience of the night they had all just spent. She jumped up hurriedly as a scuffle from the basket in the corner told her Quiz was going to collect the letters. It was a little task she herself had coaxed him to perform, and once he got the idea that it was his own particular job he did it with enthusiasm, that sometimes ran away with him to the extent that he stopped half way down the hall to chew his burden before bringing it to Katie. One morning he had chewed up a new cheque book into pulpy uselessness before Katie realised he was away for longer than usual, and Ross's annoyance when she handed him the remains had ensured her escorting the pup ever since, until he had reached an age of greater responsibility.

'They're mostly for Ross.' Since his own home had been unoccupied and he had come to stay at Mallets, the village postman had obligingly dropped his mail through the letter box of his temporary residence each day. 'A postcard for you and Ben.' She dropped Ross's mail on the hall table, handed Amy her card, and resumed her seat with a letter in her own hand.

'Oh, it's from my sister. She's gone to Blackpool for the week,' Amy gazed at the gaudy photograph with pleasure. 'Who's yours from, Miss Katie?'

Katie could not take offence at her innocent inquiry, rather she welcomed it, for it meant sharing. She missed her family for that reason. Since she had come to Mallets she had felt very much alone, cut off from the friendly give and take of her everyday life, and experiencing for the first time the soul-destroying isolation of being among strangers, and unwelcome.

'It's from Mark, the envelope's in his handwriting.' She slit it open and her smile brightened. 'From Wyn too, she's taken over the other sheet. Oh, it's a boy!' Her eyes shone. 'He's six pounds something or other—I can't read that bit, and they've named him Shrimp because he's all pink and creased. Oh, the horrid pair!' she laughed, her eyes dancing with delight, and her own face flushed the same rosy hue as her nephew.

'That means they'll soon be able to travel.' Ross appeared in the doorway, towelling himself dry. Katie could hear Ben sluicing himself with noisy enjoyment in the scullery behind.

'Wyn says in a week or two,' she referred to the letter. 'When the baby's a month old, we'll join you, she says. That'll be in about three weeks' time,' she calculated. 'He's just six days old today.'

'He must have been born on the first day of the month—it'll be an easy birthday to remember,' Ross smiled. 'And I can hand over my—er—responsibilities to your brother by the end of the month,' he added quietly.

Katie looked up at him sharply. Did he include her among them? she wondered bleakly. Would he be so glad to be rid of her that he was counting the days until the end of the month? As she slid into bed later, her elation at the news of the baby's arrival was overlaid by sudden depression at Ross's reaction. It was good to feel the cool embrace of the sheets, she thought, as she snuggled between them gratefully. She pulled them up to her chin and turned with her back to the window, reluctant to draw the curtains and shut out the precious daylight that in itself seemed a form of security; nothing seemed quite so bad, she thought, once it was daylight. But need Ross have sounded quite so glad to be rid of his responsibilities? Even if he regarded her as one of them?

She flushed under the friendly cover of the sheets, and tried to look at things more reasonably. After all, when Mark took over it would mean that Ross could return to his own home. To look after someone else's farm as well as your own was no light task, even her sketchy knowledge of farming was enough to tell her that, and since she had been at Mallets Ross had worked from daylight to dark most days. He must be feeling the strain despite the fact that he was young and strong, and would be correspondingly glad to hand over Mark's inheritance to its proper owner to look after. The thought of Mallets without Ross was untenable, and she distracted her thoughts by concentrating on the arrival of her family. I'll have to make sure Quiz is well behaved by the time they get here, it only leaves three weeks...

The thought remained with her as she went to sleep, and she voiced it when she went into the study to collect her sketch book, and found Ross at the desk dealing with the mail she had left him that morning.

'You've got twenty-four and a half days to finish training him,' he retorted crisply, directing Katie's eyes to the wall calendar above the desk with his raised pen. She frowned. He had already crossed the first six days off. The crossings had not been on the calendar last night, or she would have noticed them. She glanced at the pen. He was using blue ink, which matched the marks on the calendar, and the last of these still shone faintly wet. He must be more eager than she had realised to leave Mallets, she thought, her spirits dropping.

'The roof of the Lodge will be finished by then.' It seemed an obvious comment, but she didn't know what else to say, and she dared not voice what she was really thinking, particularly to Ross. He was the last person to whom she could confide her misery.

'They're well on schedule,' he agreed. 'If you're going down there to take photographs,' he indicated the camera slung about her shoulder; she had told him of her intention as being a handy thing to talk about during their long wait overnight, 'I'll come with you for the walk.'

'I thought you were going to bed?' she objected. It would be wonderful to have Ross with her, and yet ... She reached out eagerly for the opportunity, and shrank from the pain of it at the same time.

'I went to bed this morning, the same as you,' Ross explained. 'Ben insisted on staying up to do the first shift. The bull knows him better than he knows me, and I think he's spent most of the morning talking to him over the door of his stall. He's fed him, too, and that finally did the trick, I think. He's calmed down enough to be able to leave.'

'He's still locked up, isn't he?' Katie's voice was apprehensive.

'Yes, I'll not risk him outside again until tomorrow,' Ross responded. 'But if anything goes wrong Ben's within call, Amy is up and she can rouse him if necessary. I've warned Eve, so she'll make sure her early pupils don't go into the yard for any reason.'

Despite his tiredness, he'd been in touch with Eve. A pang shot through Katie, and she winced, although common sense told her that it was a necessary precaution. She would be the last one to wish her own experience of the night on to another person, even Eve.

'I'm ready when you are,' she said dully. 'I'll go and fetch Quiz.'

'In that case we'll have to go separately. I want to take the goat with us and let him into the field with the sheep.' Ross stamped the last envelope and gathered them together preparatory to leaving them on the hall table. 'After the way I've trained him, that billy doesn't think much of dogs, and I don't particularly want him to tangle with Quiz. The pup's a lot too young, and he might get damaged,' he added.

'Then I'll leave him here,' Katie decided. She could not forgo the hours with Ross, even if she had to make a third with the goat, she decided wryly. 'You're not letting him follow us loose, like that?' Her eyes widened as Ross walked up to the railed enclosure in the yard and pulled it apart to let the animal through. 'What if . . . ?' She gulped. She felt she had had enough of wild beasts for one day.

'He's quite harmless,' Ross smiled, handing the expected titbit to the animal, which munched happily, and fell into line behind them as meekly as if he was Ross's dog.

'Where's Glen?' She glanced round fearfully in case the retriever followed them and a fracas started.

'In the house with Quiz.' Ross's smile broadened. 'I promise you the goat won't charge,' he said teasingly. 'If I can rescue you from a bull I'm sure I'm quite capable of dealing with a billygoat.' He took her hand gaily, and her instant, nervous grip turned his smile into a grin, which brought the ready colour to her cheeks, deepened by her own annoyance that it had given her away.

'What about the ponies?' She indicated Eve's small herd in the next paddock.

'We shall miss those if we go out this way.' He turned her through the first gate instead of the second one which she usually took to go down to the brook. 'It'll only mean a diversion of a couple of fields, and it's a nice day for a walk,' he said contentedly. 'By the way, do you ride?' as he noticed her interest in the ponies.

'No. I've always thought I'd like to, but somehow I've never had the opportunity,' she responded wistfully.

'Then we'll have to make time for you to get a ride or two in—there won't be an opportunity for much longer,' he responded generously. 'This way.' He herded the goat through the gate, and closed it as soon as Katie was safely through. She would have liked to ride. There were one or two adult-sized horses in the paddock as well as the ponies that the children rode, but she had no desire to be taught by Eve, and from what Ross had said it looked as if the riding school mistress would be giving up her business when she and Ross were married. Probably the fact that she would have to vacate the fields she leased at Mallets when Mark took over had helped to accelerate the marraige. The thought did not make Katie feel any happier, and she jumped nervously as she felt a soft muzzle prospecting her hand.

'He only wants a titbit,' Ross smiled. 'Give him this.' He handed her a piece of sweet biscuit rather the worse for wear from being in his pocket, but evidently kept there for that purpose, and she held it out gingerly. 'What did I tell you? He's quite friendly,' but just the same Ross kept hold of her hand as they walked down the slope of the field, with the billy following behind them. Katie resisted an almost pathological urge to look over her shoulder, determined not to give Ross another opportunity to jibe, but her rear felt more than vulnerable, and she congratulated herself that she was not in her red trouser suit. To her knowledge the colour did not offend goats, but it was nicer to be on the safe side.

'This is where I leave you.' Ross addressed the goat gravely as they entered a field where a flock of ewes and lambs grazed peacefully. 'You stay here, Katie,' he went on, opening the gate and allowing the goat to follow him through. 'I'm coming back in a minute. Here you are, old chap.' He bent down and sprinkled biscuit bits among the grass over an area covered by the arc of his arm, and with a pat on its horny head he left the goat following the trail of sweetmeats, and steadily browsing towards the flock it was there to guard. Ross retraced his steps, and absentmindedly took Katie's hand in his own again, turning to shut the gate with his other. 'Now for the Lodge. The light should be good for your photography.' He glanced up at the almost cloudless sky.

'I hope the weather's like this when Mark and Wyn arrive,' she commented. 'First impressions make such a difference, and Mallets has always been a bit of a bogey to us, ever since we were children,' she confessed.

'Now he's coming to live here, I want him to like it, right from the start.' It would be awful if he didn't, and felt he had to carry on living there because it would eventually become his son's inheritance. She put the thought from her; it was no good jumping those sorts of hurdles until they appeared.

'First impressions *are* important, but they aren't everything,' Ross answered quietly. 'They can be overlaid by others, when you get to know a—a place.' Had he meant to say 'a person'? He spoke carefully, as if he was choosing his words. Choosing to remain on friendly terms with her, conscious that her family would soon be here, and wanting to start on the right footing with his new neighbours-to-be?

He needn't worry so far as I'm concerned, she thought wearily; she was too tired to wish to quarrel with anyone at the moment. And he was correct in what he said. Her own impressions had been overlaid by others, certainly so far as Ross himself was concerned. She had disliked him before she even met him, resenting his position at the farm that had been upheld by the solicitor despite her objections, but even in such unfertile soil her love had grown and flourished, against her own will, for it would have been easier for her if she could have remained heartwhole. Now, after last night, she probably owed him her life as well. She

226

sighed.

His hand fumbled in his pocket, and came towards her with a coin on the flat on his palm.

'This for your thoughts?'

Katie looked down at the small brown disc of the penny he offered her, and sudden tears pricked her eyes. A childish bribe for her secrets. She shook her head, not wanting to look at him.

'They're worth—much more.' Her voice caught on the words, and she turned away from him, looking backwards, pretending to be searching for the goat they had left in the field behind them. 'I can't see him, can you?' She couldn't see anything except a hazy blur, but her ploy worked, and diverted Ross's interest for the moment.

'Yes, he's joined the flock—look,' he put the penny back in his pocket and pointed. 'He'll graze with them, for company, and I'll know the sheep have got a twenty-four-hour watch with them. He shows up well among the white wool, doesn't he?'

'Yes, you'll be able to pick him out when you want him,' she agreed numbly, somehow finding her voice again, even if she had to tell him a white lie about seeing the goat. Her normally keen sight was foiled by tears, and as she turned back to resume their walk she brushed them aside hastily, so that Ross should not see, for he would surely demand

227

to know why she was crying when she had every reason to be glad with the news she had received from her family that morning.

'Steady over the plank.' He put out a hasty hand to hold her as she stepped blindly on to the makeshift bridge over the brook, and stumbled, not seeing clearly where she was going. 'One adventure in a day is quite enough,' he admonished her, putting a steadying arm about her waist, and keeping it there as they turned onto the path beside the brook, watching for the uneven ruts left there by rain and the wheels of farm machinery. Katie rested in the circle of his arm, briefly, luxuriously. Painfully, so that with an effort she pulled herself away, denying her heart, that yearned for her to remain where she was, sheltered by the protection she most longed for, but could not have unless it was accompanied by his love, and that was not her right to claim.

'If the thatcher's finished doing the well in the yard, I'd like a photograph of that. A thatched well's unusual.' She took refuge in the job she had come to do. 'You carry on, if you want to see the man,' she excused him from accompanying her. 'I can find my own way about. Only in the garden, of course,' she added hastily, lest he should think she had been prying about his home.

'Haven't you been inside the house?' Ross nodded to the thatcher cheerfully, but made

228

no move to join him, remaining by Katie's side as she made her way towards the yard behind the house. 'You must have a look round before we go back, it's interesting inside,' he invited. 'Now, whereabouts do you want to stand to get your picture?' as they approached the well. 'It looks good now it's newly thatched.' He glanced at the craftsman's work appreciatively.

'About here, I think.' Katie hesitated, and succumbed. 'It would be better if someone sat on the edge.' She despised herself for her tactics, but the urge to have one photograph of Ross to keep was too much even for her self-discipline. It's not much to ask, she excused herself, and smiled as he obligingly sat on the edge of the brickwork in the spot she indicated. 'Just one more, in case that one comes out blurred.' She used every amateur photographer's excuse to click another one, aided as such excuses always are by the fact she had over twenty more snaps still unexposed in her camera. 'There, that's fine.'

'You've wasted a perfectly good snap,' Ross teased. 'The first one would have come out clearly enough. What'll you do with two?' He rose and looked down at her, and she dropped her eyes to the camera, twiddling unnecessarily with the reading. 'Or do you live by the principle of "one to keep and one to give away"?' His eyes were laughing, and she smiled in answer, but the smile only touched her lips, her brown eyes remained bleak. Was he hinting that he would like the duplicate snap himself, to give away? To Eve?

'I took the second one from a slightly different angle,' she defended her action, determined that even if there was not a pin's difference between the two photographs, she could not—would not—release one of them to be given to Eve. The riding mistress would have Ross himself, what did she want with his photograph as well?

'If you've finished, come and have a look at the inside of the house,' he repeated his invitation, taking her arm and strolling towards the almost completed Lodge. 'The furniture's all in dust sheets in the stables,' he waved his arm at the solidly bolted doors, 'you can have a peep at that another time. I imagine some of the pieces might interest you.' She had expressed delight in some of the furnishings in her grandfather's home, and flatteringly he remembered her interest, although this was not surprising since it was aligned closely with his own taste, which would make it an easy thing to remember, even to a disinterested stranger, she thought, wondering when he imagined she might look at his furniture. Certainly not after he and Eve were married—she could not believe an invitation would come her way from the auburn-haired girl, who had made her dislike of Katie apparent from the first. And if Ross invited her, and his wife did not second it, she could always, when she was staying with Mark and Wyn, make an excuse to babysit with her small nephew while his parents went instead. The thought comforted her. She could not imagine never coming to stay with her family, but if staying with them meant meeting Ross and his wife the erstwhile treasured times with her family would become more pain than pleasure, she thought.

'The door's already open, Mr Heseltine.' The thatcher saw them approach, divined their intention and saved Ross the necessity of searching for his key.

'Right, thanks,' he responded pleasantly. 'We shan't be long, only Miss Kimberley wants to look inside.' She didn't. It was Ross who had invited her, not Katie who had asked, but it seemed a waste of time to point this out and she remained silent, waiting while he opened the studded front door of the house, the one she had leaned her back against on the day when she first realised she loved its owner. It opened noiselessly, swinging on large hinges, and Ross stood aside for her to enter, waiting courteously while she crossed the threshold of what was to be another woman's home.

CHAPTER TEN

'They're in the house, miss.'

The thatcher's voice floated through the open doorway, and light footsteps—those of a woman—tapped on the path outside.

'I'll find them, don't bother to come down.' It was Eve's voice, cool and crisp, cutting across Ross's quiet explanation to Katie of the work he was having done, and to which she listened avidly, not so much to hear what he was saying as for the joy of hearing the deep, precious tones of his voice.

'Ross, are you there? Where are you?' The studded door swung wide and rapped sharply against the opposite wall, the hand that pushed it careless of the damage to panelling and door alike.

'In here, Eve,' Ross directed her, but he remained where he was beside Katie, and she looked up at him in surprise, wondering at the faint frown that flickered across his face, and was instantly gone as he turned to greet the newcomer. He was probably wishing he was here on his own, thought Katie wretchedly, feeling instantly superfluous now that Eve had come, her enjoyment ruined, because despite her own tempestuous feelings she *was* enjoying looking round the Lodge with Ross. The rooms were spacious, but not so big that they lost their cosy feel, and the improvements Ross was having done while his furniture was being stored caught her interest. She liked old buildings, and when Ross had finished with it, this one would still retain its beauty, and yet unobtrusively include those amenities that made modern living a pleasant and convenient thing, and which had always made Katie, who loved the treasures of the past, glad that she had been born in the present age, and envious now of the woman who would be mistress in this lovely house, and thereby able to have both, as well as spend the rest of her life with the man who now stood at Katie's side.

'One of the ponies has gone lame, and Ben's not around.' Eve's eyebrows rose as she saw that Katie was with Ross, and that, moreover, he still held her hand; he had grasped it to guide her across the step of the door, guarding her against a stumble in the room that seemed dim after the brightness of the sunshine outside.

'I know all the pitfalls here,' he smiled. 'There are steps and things in unexpected places, and we don't want an accident.'

Probably he didn't want to be saddled with her presence for any longer than was absolutely necessary, and if she ricked an ankle and was confined to the house he might feel it was his duty to remain and keep her company. The possibility made the thought of a ricked ankle a pleasurable thing, and she put it aside as being unworthy; such methods were best left to people like Eve.

'Ben's in bed. Is there anything I can do?' Ross's voice was quiet, concerned for her problem.

'In bed? At this time of day?' Eve's voice was incredulous. She made being in bed in the afternoon sound like a crime, thought Katie scornfully; she condemned before she had discovered the reason.

'We've been up all night with the bull.' Ross didn't enlarge, and Katie cast him a grateful glance.

'Oh, Amy bumbled on about the bull when I went up to the house.' Eve's voice was cutting. 'She said you'd frightened it, or something,' she directed a withering look at Katie. 'If you don't understand the stock, why don't you keep away from them?' she criticised sharply. 'That sort of behaviour can cost someone else their life.'

'It was no one's fault. It was mischance that could happen to anybody.' Ross's voice was unexpectedly firm and he moved towards the door, dropping Katie's hand, and leaving her to follow him. For a moment she stood undecided. If they had been outside in the garden she would have remained where she was, on the pretext of taking more photographs, but she could not very well remain here in Ross's house without his permission, and if she asked for that there was no doubt he would think it a peculiar request, and want to know the reason why.

'I'll come back with you and have a look at the pony,' he offered. 'You've finished here, haven't you, Katie?' He turned back to her, his hand already on the knob of the door, politely waiting for her to join them. The clear sunlight fell on Eve and Ross standing together in the doorway, the tall lean figure of the man, and the slender, auburn-haired woman. They make a handsome couple, thought Katie wistfully, feeling her own colouring to be dowdy and insignificant beside Eve's.

'Yes, I've finished.' She could not very well say otherwise, since she had already told him she had got sufficient snaps for her purpose at the moment, and refusing his offer to help her take more since she could not bear his kindly teasing. It no longer annoyed her, it just hurt, and her bruised feelings protested that they would accept no more. She followed him to the door, paused on the step beside him and she saw him run exploring fingers over the panelling on the wall behind, where it had struck when Eve opened it to come in to them. 'Has it done any damage?' She couldn't resist the question, although she told herself that it was no business of hers. 'You need a wedge under the door.' She hated to see anything ill-used, and the panelling in the

Lodge was particularly lovely, the wood grain glowing from decades of polishing until it shone with a heart in it that only generations of care can give.

'There's normally a leather "dog" there to stop the door from going back too far,' Ross responded, quietly shutting it behind him, 'but it was put into the stables with the rest of the furniture until the roof's finished. It hasn't marked the wood, though, it's oak, and that's tough,' he added thankfully.

'I can't think why you don't have all that gloomy panelling ripped out,' Eve said carelessly. 'You might as well, now you're having the place done up, and have some cheerful wallpaper put there instead. I hate dark rooms,' she screwed up her face expressively, and Katie winced. So much for the panelling! She had no doubt that Ross would do as Eve said, after all she would soon be mistress of the Lodge, and it was her right to have the house as she liked it, but Katie mourned for the beautiful old woodwork.

'It isn't dark really, the windows are huge,' she made a valiant effort to save it. 'After all, it's only half panelled, the walls are plain from there to the ceiling. You could use wallpaper instead of emulsion on the top half of the walls. That is, if you really wanted to.' Her voice questioned the wisdom of such a move. Ross had said he had kept one or two nice pictures that were favourites of his parents, and she imagined they would be of the kind that would show up well on plain walls. The thought of what Eve described as 'cheerful wallpaper' made her shudder. In a nursery or domestic quarters, yes, but not in that lovely big living room. Furnished properly—and Katie had no doubt that his furniture would blend to make a harmonious, restful place that at its best such a room could be—it would have all the light it needed and more. She flushed suddenly, sensing Eve's contempt, her impatience at an outsider's interference in what she could rightly consider was no concern of Katie's. She did not see the quiet regard of two blue eyes a distance above her head, that rested on its gold-tipped covering with a guarded look as if it would ask a question, but hesitated, and when Eve spoke again the opportunity was lost.

'It's the new pony that's gone lame. I'm beginning to wish I hadn't bought the thing.' Katie felt sorry for the pony. Granted that Eve was running the riding school as a business, and for her living, just the same her 'tools' were flesh and blood, and surely even if the pony was a new one, it had a name? And if the pony was lame, why didn't Eve see to it herself? She was quite capable, Katie knew, she had seen her checking the animals on her own before. Doubtless Amy had told her that Ross had come to the Lodge with

Katie and she had come deliberately to disturb them.

'It's probably just a stone. Let's go and have a look.' Ross strode along the back of the brook with Eve beside him, his one hand—the one which had held Katie's—deep in his pocket. Eve had no trouble keeping up with him, she was taller than Katie, who had to walk at her best pace to remain with the others, but she was determinedly just behind them when they reached the plank bridge.

'The children have moved it again.' Eve clicked her tongue with annoyance. 'I'll read the riot act to them when I get back!' she promised ill-humouredly, and walked out unhesitatingly over the unstable plank, that rocked in the most alarming fashion as she got to the middle, and over the deepest part of the brook. For the moment Katie thought—no, she did *not* hope, she told herself firmly—that Eve would emulate Quiz and qualify for a ducking, but with a graceful sway of her body she righted herself and reached the other bank in safety.

'Your turn now.' Was there a hint of a twinkle in Ross's eye? Katie glared at him, and her chin came up, but just the same she hesitated as she felt the plank move under her feet at the first step.

'Oh, come on! Don't say you're scared of that as well,' Eve called impatiently. The contempt in her voice gave Katie's courage

238

the impetus it needed. She was scared, but she wouldn't admit it, and hardly daring to look where she was going she completed the crossing at a run, and landed on the opposite bank beside Eve with a gasp of relief she could not suppress.

'Well done!' Ross's voice was quiet in her ear. She imagined Eve would not hear it, because as soon as he joined them she turned and strode away again, deliberately fast, walking uphill as easily as if the ground was level, a silent taunt to Katie, who was too out of breath by the time they reached the ponies to even voice a protest.

'This is the one—bring him along, Emma,' Eve called, and the small pigtailed Brownie obeyed, leading the limping pony towards them.

'I fink he's got a stone in his hoof ...' she began, and Eve rounded on her sharply.

'That's for me to say. Mr Heseltine is going to have a look at him—' she checked herself with a quick glance towards Ross. Katie felt sure if he had not been there she would not have done so, and her pupil flushed unhappily.

'Let me have a look at him,' Ross spoke kindly to the little girl, who responded with a smile, as he bent down in front of the animal's forehoof. 'Hold this for me while I see to him, Katie.' He drew his hand from his pocket and held it over her own, and she felt

239

something small and light drop into her palm. She looked down. It was the penny, the one he had offered her for her thoughts earlier, a silent jibe, daring her to voice the feelings that must have been evident in her face, and to judge from this reaction, to be causing him amusement. She flushed as scarlet as Emma, and felt a small hand take her own on the other side. Fellow feeling, she thought, her sense of humour restoring her colour to near normal, but not before Eve had directed a malicious smile at her, penetrating the reason for her flush, and from her superior standing with Ross not caring, thought Katie furiously.

'Will you have to miss your riding lesson?' The small fingers clutching her own gave her an excuse to divert her attention from where Ross and Eve knelt together to examine the pony's hoof, the dark head and the auburn one closely side by side. Surely Eve need not get so close, thought Katie. Her hair as she bent over the hoof was getting in Ross's way, and he pushed it aside with a smile that brought an answering one from the girl, who tossed it back across her shoulders with a provocative movement, and Katie looked away with a grimace of distaste, and became conscious that her young companion was talking to her.

'It'll soon be too late for a lesson, I've got to be home for tea time.' Emma's lips drooped, and Katie squeezed her hand sympathetically; the disappointment of a missed ride would loom large for a small girl.

'Never mind, it's your Brownie meeting tomorrow night,' a flash of memory inspired her. 'There's always the Brownie meeting,' she consoled, conscious that there would soon be another disappointment for Emma when Eve gave up her riding school after her marriage to Ross.

'There won't always be the Brownie meetings.' The lips drooped lower still. 'Brown Owl says when it's winter we won't be able to use our own hut.' The local Cubs and Brownie pack boasted a wooden hut of their own on the edge of the local playing fields. It was an amenity jealously guarded, because it housed their assortment of toadstools, camping equipment, and, Katie did not doubt, the stuffed owl that she herself had donated, and a large lock on the door gave aggressive assurance to the small fry who regarded it as their exclusive property that their treasures were safe against all intruders.

'Why? Isn't it heated?' Katie wondered idly how they had managed to cope during previous winters.

'Oh yes, it's lovely and warm, we've got a big stove,' Emma assured her, 'but the roof leaks an' Brown Owl says there's not enough money to mend it wiv,' she explained disconsolately.

'What a shame!' It did seem a pity, their small hut meant a lot to them, and the village hall wouldn't really be suitable. It was too big, which would make the cost of the overheads for such small meetings prohibitive unless they were subsidised, and Katie appreciated that in such a small community funds would be scarce, and any available money would have a list of higher priorities than Brownie meetings.

'Perhaps someone will manage to find enough money before the winter starts,' she tried to cheer Emma up. What the children really needed was an interested philanthropist. Someone with a stake in the community, and money they didn't need. A legacy, or ... A happy thought struck her. She could solve Emma's problem herself. At least her own legacy would make someone happy, she thought, with a touch of bitterness that passed as quickly as it came. In a way, she would have a stake in the community, in the shape of her family. One day, perhaps, her infant nephew might belong to the Cub pack. The thought brought a quick pricking behind her eyes, and she blinked. It would have been wonderful if her own son or daughter could belong as well. Her own and Ross's children. She forced the thought from her mind, and looked down at the freckled face below her. 'I'm sure we'll be able to think of something,' she told it, with such

242

confidence that a beam of delight transformed the drooping lips into a wide curved smile, and made her glad that she had the certain means to do something about her implied promise. The total trust in the child's face made her pause, appreciating the import of her brother's letter, and his expressed sense of responsibility for the new life he had helped to create, at which she had laughed at first. 'He'll get over it,' she had chuckled, reading it aloud to Amy, but now, soberly, she felt she knew what he meant, and she no longer felt inclined to laugh.

I'll go and see Jeremy Bailey tomorrow, she promised herself, grateful that for the second time Emma had unwittingly provided her with a solution to a problem. A means of disposal of unwanted goods, thought Katie. A dustbin, really, but it wasn't quite like that, because the small Brownie and her pack would be as glad of the stuffed owl, and the money to mend their roof, as Katie was glad to get rid of them.

'I'll have to go, Miss Clements, it's nearly tea time.' Emma spoke hesitatingly, obviously torn between awe of her riding mistress and obedience to her mother's injunction to be home for tea.

'Run along, then,' Eve said carelessly, without bothering to look up, and the child skipped away with a cheerful wave to Katie and not even a backward glance towards her riding mistress, who had risen to her feet beside Ross, and was brushing her hands together after helping him to hold the pony's hoof. For such a small pony it seemed unnecessary for two people to have to hold its hoof, Katie thought bitingly, but she made no comment as the other two strolled towards her, Ross folding a tool from his all-purpose knife back into the handle as he walked.

'It was just a stone, as Emma said,' he spoke casually, 'but the shoe doesn't fit very well. I'd have the blacksmith look at him if I were you.'

'I might as well while I've got the opportunity,' Eve responded, and this time there was a bite in her voice, and it wasn't directed at Katie. Or at Ross. It was just there, an undercurrent that Katie sensed but could not place. Perhaps Eve resented having to give up her riding school after her marriage, although Katie would not have thought Ross would object to her having an interest to occupy her while he was busy about his estate. A riding school would be a tie, though; it meant set hours for lessons, and a seven-day week responsibility for the animals which might not accord with Ross's plans for their home life. She'd do better if she took up painting, thought Katie. That could be more easily fitted in to the life style the artist chose to adopt. It would have been so easy if she instead of Eve was marrying

Ross...

'It's no good daydreaming about things that aren't going to happen, she told herself firmly the next morning, as she got ready to depart for the village on her mission to see the solicitor.

'I'd better ring him first.' She had mentioned her intention to Ross, though not the reason for it.

'If he can see you, you can come with me. I've got to go and collect the tyre I left. It'll save you waiting for the bus,' Ross offered. 'The garage said it would be ready in twenty-four hours, and it's over that now.'

'Heavens, is it only a day since you went to the darts match with Ben?' It seemed like a hundred years, so much had happened, and the news about her nephew's arrival had made it seem even longer.

'You'll get used to these upheavals on a farm,' Ross smiled. 'It becomes just a part of the routine after a while.'

She wouldn't get used to them. She dialled the solicitor's number savagely, forcing herself to concentrate on what she was doing so that she need not look at Ross, nor think about what he was saying. She wouldn't ever be at Mallets long enough to get used to rural upheavals. After she had spent a short time helping Mark and Wyn to settle in she'd accept one of the several commissions she had been offered—preferably one that took her

245

farthest away from Little Twickenham, out of the country if possible—and she could leave all this, and the memory of Ross, behind her.

'It'll all add to the interest of the book you're illustrating.' Ross still stood behind her, the familiar, teasing note in his voice.

'I'd forgotten about that.' She had. She would have to remain in the locality until she had finished what she had promised to do. Bitterly she regretted her impulse, but it was too late now; she had had a phone call from the publisher that morning enthusiastically accepting her offer of illustrations, and giving her a free hand within the subject matter of the book to deal with it as she chose.

'Bother! That's twice I've misdialled.' She put the receiver down and waited for the dialling tone to reappear.

'Still jittery?' Ross smiled, and took it from her hand. 'Let me do it for you, I know Jeremy Bailey's number.' He dialled with firm, sure strokes of a brown index finger, listened for a while, then handed the phone to Katie. 'It's all yours,' he said quietly. 'Let me know if you have any luck. I'll wait for you outside.'

He turned and strode through the door, leaving her the privacy of the hall in which to do her talking, a courtesy that was natural to Ross, and which she had liked in him from the start.

'Yes, Mr Bailey's free, Miss Kimberley,

any time during the morning,' the clerk's friendly voice assured her, and she put the receiver down, thankful that at least she could start something positive moving in this one direction. Anything else she undertook seemed fraught with unexpected pitfalls, she thought ruefully, but over this one thing at least she had the means of control.

'Any time during the morning,' she told Ross, joining him on the doorstep as soon as she had finished.

'In that case, come along with me to collect the tyre. You can call on the solicitor on the way back, and I'll wait for you. Unless you're going to stay with him for lunch this time?' he questioned quietly. Katie flushed, the gall of that other, painful day still bitter.

'No, we'll be back for lunch. Amy's serving it cold so the time won't matter particularly.' She kept her voice even, refusing to be goaded, bending to ruffle Quiz's ears as he trotted through the door after her, patently begging to go along as well.

'Bring him if you like,' Ross offered generously. 'I'll look after him while you're in the solicitor's office.' He did not ask her what she was going for, respecting her privacy in the same way she would have respected his, and contrarily she wished he wouldn't. If only he would do something to make her dislike him again, it would make life much easier. Suddenly the rest of the month until Mark

247

arrived to take over seemed a very long time. Twenty-four and a half days, Ross had said. There were only twenty-three of them left now, and the last one had seemed like a lifetime. She picked up the puppy, automatically letting it chew her thumb until she caught Ross's eyes on her, and pulled it away, surreptitiously giving it the leather strap of her handbag instead.

'Give him this, it's less expensive.' Ross settled himself into the driving seat and handed her the pup's rubber ball, and she took it from him shamefacedly.

'I didn't stop to find it,' she confessed. She hadn't wanted to keep him waiting, although he seemed prepared to wait for her while she was at the solicitor's.

'I've found a use for the money Grandfather left me.' She felt she owed him some explanation, otherwise he might think she was going to the solicitor to complain about something. 'I don't want it, and it might as well be put to use in the village,' she finished, having given him the gist of what she intended, briefly and in a crisp, businesslike tone that denied any personal feelings in the matter.

'You'd be better rid of it, if you don't want to keep it,' Ross answered her quietly when she finished. 'You'd get no joy from it, the origin of it would always be there, in the background.' His tone told her that he

248

understood, even approved what she was doing. That makes a change! thought Katie with a flash of wry humour, but she felt glad she had told him. His approval didn't matter, she would have done it just the same, but somehow it helped. And it told her something else about Ross, that money as such meant very little to him. 'You'll be better rid of it,' as if it was so much rubbish, to be jettisoned to make room for something worthwhile. Her own point of view exactly, and she relaxed in the seat beside him and began to enjoy the calm, easy progression of the vehicle through the lovely countryside, for Ross seemed in no mood to hurry, and kept a gentle pace, safer through the high-banked, twisting lanes, and more enjoyable through such glorious scenery. The wolds had much to offer those who lived and worked among them, she thought wistfully, regretting her own imminent departure for that reason as well as others, for during the short stay Katie had taken the soft, rounded hills and low green valleys to her heart, and would have been more than content to make such loveliness her home.

'I'm sorry about the bull.' It had come out, and now she had started on explanations, she might as well go on. There might not be another such opportunity, when the two of them had this kind of privacy, she thought, screwing her courage together to broach the subject.

'Sorry—why?' He sounded genuinely puzzled.

'It was my fault Cup was frightened, and he could have hurt you or Ben.' Her voice was small. Eve's words still rankled, the truth of them rubbing abrasively at her conscience so that by the time the sleepless night was over and the morning came again she felt almost as badly as if Ross or Ben had really been hurt in the affray, instead of simply losing a night's sleep, and they had all done that.

'You were doing me a favour by locking up,' he pointed out, seeming in no way disturbed by the subject. 'And it would have been just the same if Ben or I had held the lantern—the bull would have been as frightened of his own shadow no matter who was behind the light. Perhaps not if it had been Ben, he's known him all his life, and talks to him like a baby,' Ross smiled. 'But I don't think I could have calmed him myself, he hasn't known me much longer than he's known you.'

'Eve said ...' she began hesitantly.

'Take no notice of what Eve said.' Momentarily his own voice was as sharp as that habitually used by the riding mistress. 'She had no means of knowing what lay behind the uproar.' His voice was gentle again. 'Just be thankful none of us was hurt.'

'Thankful ...?' Katie stared at him, shocked into silence. To be thankful for such as night as that...!

'I am—in a way,' Ross said quietly, pulling up at the crossroads at the entrance to the village.

'Mind the trader's van!' Katie couldn't help it, she felt she could not stand another fright just yet, and the trader's van was looming up with alarming speed.

'He's going round the green.' The van turned as if in obedience to his words, and Katie breathed freely again. 'We're going straight on, the garage is on the other side of the village.' He did not even tease, and Katie relaxed in her seat again, calm enough to respond to the infant growls of the pup in her arms that dared her to take its ball from between the teeth that had so recently chewed her thumb. She played with the little animal absentmindedly, only half conscious of what she was doing, thinking over the words Ross had just spoken. 'I am—in a way.' That was twice he had said something similar, she thought wonderingly, puzzled at what good think could come from spending the night calming an infuriated bull, with the frail prongs of a pitchfork the only things between himself and the possibility of a hideous death.

'You were pretty frank about what you thought of me, when I was up on the beam,' she reminded him, remembering his blunt comments then.

'I had to be,' he responded calmly. 'I daren't let you go to sleep up there, and by being thoroughly unpleasant to you, I was able to make you angry enough to stay awake. Didn't you realise that?'

'I thought you meant it . . .' Her voice was small, a strange, stifled feeling making her suddenly breathless, so that she was unable to finish what she wanted to say.

'Well, I'm . . . what a horror you must think me!' Ross laughed out loud. 'Hello, John. We've come for the tyre.' He slid the window open and leaned out, calling to a mechanic who strolled onto the garage forecourt wiping his hands on an oily rag.

'I've got it here, Mr Heseltine. Stay where you are,' as Ross made to get out. 'I'll drop it in the back for you, and you can settle with the boss when you pay your petrol bill,' he called cheerfully, heaving the heavy wheel with no apparent effort into the back of their vehicle with a thump that brought a quick yap from Quiz and a grin to the mechanic's face when he saw the size of the yapper.

'Nice little feller,' he said approvingly. 'He'll make you a good guard dog when he's grown,' he told Katie seriously.

'He's not mine, really.' The wistful tone brought Ross's eyes round to her sharply, but she was bending over Quiz, easing the ball out from under him where it had rolled on to the seat as he jumped up when the thump of the wheel startled him, and she did not see.

'There's another one in the kennels.' Ross resumed their conversation when they were on their way back to the village again, and Katie looked at him for a moment, uncomprehendingly. 'Another pup like Quiz,' he enlarged patiently. 'You're going to miss him, aren't you?' He spared her a glance as they reached the crossroads again and they pulled up cautiously on the otherwise deserted thoroughfare. 'Why not keep him,' Ross suggested gently, 'and we can get the other pup for your brother. It hurts, parting with dogs,' he acknowledged, with the fellow feeling of all dog owners.

'I'd like to.' Katie fondled the small ears, risked Ross's displeasure and let him chew her thumb. 'But it's no good, I can't keep a dog.' How could she travel with Quiz? A lot of her assignments were abroad, and if she brought him back with her he would spend more time in quarantine than he did with her. It was not fair on the dog, he would be better left with her brother and his family. That way he would have the child to play with and all the freedom of the farm, a halcyon life for a small dog. No, he would be best left behind. 'What are you stopping for?' She realised in a bemused way that they were stationary, and Ross was switching off the engine.

'I thought you wanted to go and see the

solicitor?' There was a deep, amused smile in his eyes, and Katie flushed.

'I didn't realise we were here.' She turned to the door hastily, and he grabbed her.

'Mind the van!' He loosed her slowly as it shot past round the green, and she fled across the road and into the solicitor's office without a backward glance.

'It's as good as done,' she said when she rejoined him half an hour later, 'and he promised that it would be given as an anonymous gift,' she said thankfully. 'He gave me a lot of good advice about investing it and drawing the income,' she remembered, appreciating that the solicitor had been trying to be helpful, 'but I think in the end he was quite pleased that it would benefit the village.'

'Now you can concentrate on your own affairs.' Ross's voice held quiet satisfaction.

'Oh, those. I'll use the rest of the month to get the illustrations for that book,' Katie supposed, 'and then when Mark and Wyn are settled I'll take on an assignment. I've got several lined up.' Her voice was less than enthusiastic, but she supposed it was what he wanted to know. She would soon be safely out of his way, although once Mark was here he had no need to feel responsible for her any longer, she thought tartly. 'There's the blacksmith,' she pointed out the familiar small van rocking its way wildly over the field towards the herd of ponies corralled in a corner, that came into view as they turned into the drive towards Mallets.

'I wonder if he's going to have a look at all of them,' Ross said musingly. 'It'll pay Eve to make sure they're well shod before she takes them to Wales.'

'Why Wales? Surely she could find a buyer for them nearer home?' It seemed a long way to go, to Katie, just to sell a school of riding ponies. The wolds was riding country, and there must be many willing buyers locally.

'She doesn't want to sell them. Why should she, when they're already broken in?' Ross asked. 'A riding school for young children will make an ideal extension to the pony-trekking business she's going to join, and I believe that side of it—the trekking, I mean—is already well established, and doing well. They just felt they wanted to enlarge for visitors who had got children too young to join the trekking, but liked riding. Eve had been offered the partnership before,' he added in a puzzled tone of voice, 'but she refused, goodness knows why.

Katie could have told him. But what had made Eve decide to accept the partnership now? It would take her miles away from Ross. Her head spun dizzily, so that she put one hand on the hall table for support while she picked up the letter that lay there with the other.

'It's a p.s. from Mark. He's got a head like a riddle since the baby's been born,' she smiled. 'I wonder what he wants ... oh, it's mostly for you.' She read the contents swiftly. 'Marks says to ask you if there's anything you would particularly like from Mallets, as a keepsake.' She raised sober eyes to his. 'You were a friend of Grandfather's,' she said quietly. 'There must be something? Mark says,' she referred to the letter again, '"ask Ross to choose something—will you make sure he does, Katie? We owe him a great deal, and I'm sure he'd like something that belonged to Grandfather, as a keepsake?" Mark doesn't hold any grudges, either,' she said thankfully. 'I'm glad, because it means a fresh start for the family—and for Mallets.' She cast affectionate eyes round the room that she had become fond of since she had been here. 'You seem to spend a lot of time in this room.' It was her grandfather's study. 'Perhaps there's something here?' Her eyes questioned him.

'Can I choose—anything?' His voice was hesitant, and Katie responded immediately.

'Yes, why not? Don't be put off by size.' Her grandfather's desk was a particularly beautiful piece of furniture, skilfully inlaid, and she had heard Ross comment upon it admiringly more than once. 'Something that you'd like more than anything else,' she urged him. 'Something that belonged to

Grandfather.'

'You belonged to your Grandfather.' He turned suddenly, towering over her, reaching out for her, but gently, hesitantly, as if he was not sure of her response. 'You're what I'd choose to take from Mallets, Katie—that is, if you'll come?' There was no teasing in his blue eyes now, that burned like fire with suppressed emotion, sternly held in check from consideration for her, Katie realised dimly. Waiting for her to choose, as she had waited for him. 'I asked Eve if she could guess what size your finger took.' He took her hand and held it, smilingly, in his own big one, 'but she said she didn't know. I thought all girls knew these things,' he said vaguely. That was when Eve decided to accept her partnership, thought Katie, and in her new-found happiness felt it in her heart to be sorry for the other woman. 'But it would be better if you would choose your ring—we'd do it together. I'll know you like it, then.' His voice faded uncertainly, waiting for her reaction.

'I thought you'd be glad to see me go.' Joyous laughter bubbled up inside Katie, her response writ large in her eyes, so that an answering confident smile lit his. 'When did you . . . ?'

'I think from the first time I saw you,' he answered her seriously. 'But when you were sat up on the beam in the stable, I was sure.

Oh, Katie, if the bull...'

'He didn't.' Katie put gentle fingers to his lips, stopping the words. 'But I can see now why you said you were glad it happened. I wondered—' she confessed.

'If you come home to the Lodge, you can bring Quiz,' teasingly he bribed her. 'And you've kept my penny,' he reminded her, 'so you must tell me what you're thinking.'

'They're worth much more, my thoughts,' she sighed happily, nestling into his arms, winding her own about him for as far as they would go. 'But I'll tell you, just the same...'

Photoset, printed and bound in Great Britain by REDWOOD PRESS LIMITED, Melksham, Wiltshire